Courting the Krampus

ELLE STERLING

MONSTERS OF ALBERAD

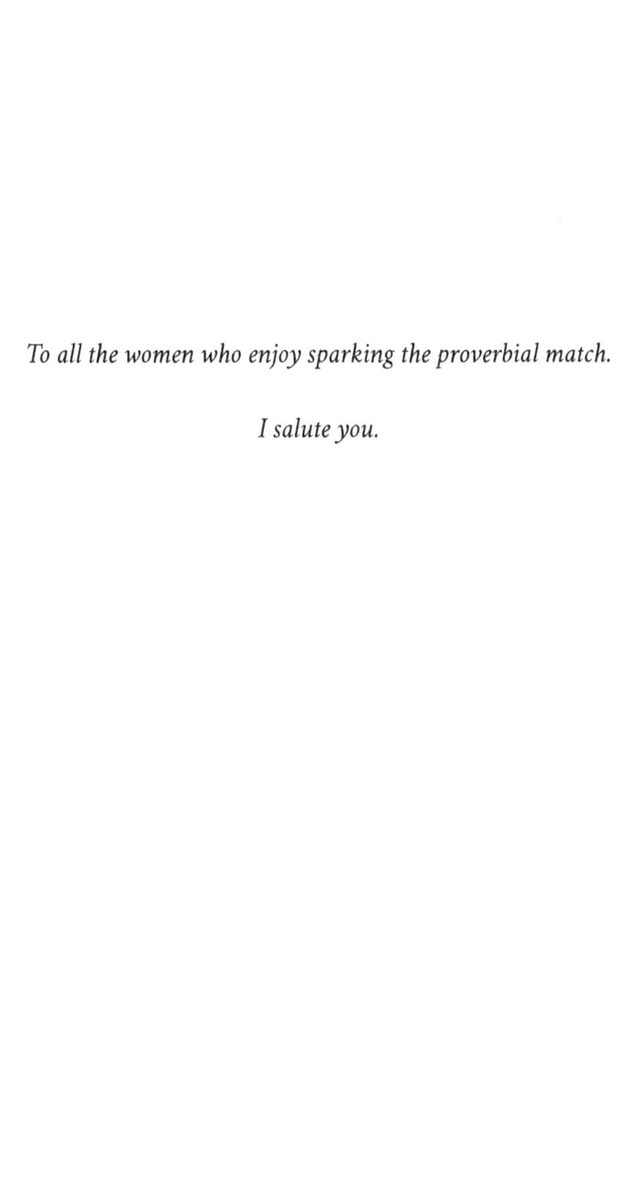

To all the women who enjoy sparking the proverbial match.

I salute you.

Natalie

"Are those anal beads?" Diana asks me, staring at the ice-blue beaded string in my hand.

"Yup," I say, unsure how cool she's going to be about me carrying around my sex toys like they're everyday accessories. I don't feel like I need to defend my choices to someone I only met yesterday, but I square my shoulders just in case the judgment train is about to hit me.

Diana sits up a bit straighter in the fancy armchair across the room, craning her neck to get a better look at the beads. I fold my hand around them, tucking them in their special pouch before dropping them in my mini backpack—the only thing I have with me besides the clothes on my body.

"Were you wearing them on the boat last night?" Curiosity laces Diana's words. She cocks her head and studies the bag as if she can see the beads through the vegan leather, the wheels evidently turning in her head.

I put my bag on the gigantic bed we had to share last night and pad over to join Diana in front of the floor-to-ceiling window, before sinking into the plush chair next to hers. I keep my gaze on the pretty sunrise across the Caribbean Sea as I contemplate what to say.

Not seeing a reason to deny the truth, I shrug and admit, "Ladies night promised to be a good time on the yacht. I thought I'd make it more fun by edging myself all night, then when I got back to my hotel—alone—I'd have some me time, if you know what I mean." I sigh at the missed opportunity, then add, "Sounded like a good plan at the time."

Diana crosses one leg over the other and scoots forward in her seat. "I don't think anyone could have predicted what happened last night."

"You mean meeting up with a group of women to sail to a supposedly uninhabited island in the middle of the Caribbean, only to stumble upon ten nonhuman beings—or 'monsters' as they call themselves—was not something you could have predicted?" I deadpan.

Diana's lips quirk. "Don't forget having a magical tattoo show up on our bodies that keeps us within a hundred yards of one of those monsters with a matching tattoo."

I laugh dryly. "Right. Not how I imagined our night would go. But it has been fun rooming with you while the monsters try to figure out how to get us off this island and back to our normal lives."

"Think we'll get to leave today?"

"As someone who didn't know magic or monsters existed yesterday, I honestly don't know how to answer." The males, as they preferred to be called since they are very much *not* men, looked even more freaked out than us human women when we discovered the magical bonds connecting us.

"You regretting all that edging now?" Diana asks playfully.

I purse my lips and angle my head to the left, then to the right, as I give it some thought.

I can't deny how tightly spun my body is. It's practically vibrating with need after having the beads hit me in all the perfect spots. I had this whole vision of going back to my hotel and taking care of myself with a couple of the toys I packed for my first trip abroad. There's nothing a dragon dildo can't fix.

My favorite one is large and a brilliant orange. It has thick veins spiraling around the shaft and an inflated bulb at its base that stretches me with the perfect amount of tension. Just thinking about it has me shifting in my seat.

"I won't say I'm regretting it. Not yet," I say. A slow smile forms on my lips as a thought sinks in. "It just means that the orgasm I'll eventually get is going to be *unbelievably* strong. But I'm so horny right now, I'm scared I might come spontaneously if someone looks at me with the slightest bit of heat in their eyes."

"Anyone? Or someone specific?" Diana teases, voice rich with mirth.

Jasper's face flashes before my eyes. That mischievous glint that's always evident in his smirk has me squirming and I squeeze my legs together, futilely trying to create some friction against my clit. I smooth the fabric of my pleated miniskirt down and trace the new tattoo on my thigh.

I don't look at Diana when I say coyly, "There's a certain someone that I wouldn't mind assisting me with this particular need."

Diana laughs and slumps into her chair. "Too bad the monster leader, Adelbert, told us we aren't allowed to touch anyone."

Narrowing my eyes, I flip my hair over my shoulder. "I don't see why not. If it's consensual and all that jazz."

I imagine Jasper pushing me up against a wall and snaking a hand under my miniskirt. He'd look so sexy with his tall form looming over me and with those thick, curly horns that are just begging to be gripped.

Jasper would have to clamp a hand over my mouth also,

because if he so much as brushes a thumb against my clit, I know I'd combust. Anyone still on the island would definitely catch us—*ugh, monster hearing*—but I don't think I'd care.

A bright blush spreads across Diana's cheeks, most likely imagining her own shenanigans. "I guess you're right. Not like I'd mind having fun with Rollo either." Her voice trails off into a whisper and she doesn't quite meet my eyes with her admission, choosing to stare at the increasingly lightening sky in the distance.

I think about Rollo, the wolf shifter whose tattoo location matches Diana's. Seeing them chatting last night, I can totally imagine them exploring options together. She doesn't seem too shy, so maybe she could get his number and they could try dating after getting off this island.

I reach between our fancy chairs and take Diana's hand. "My take is, if Adelbert can't find a fix to these bonds, and if we're going to be stuck together with these males anyway, why not make the most of it." I wink at her and she catches my drift pretty quickly.

Diana sits up and her face lightens with determination. "Right? No use worrying about tomorrow when there's so much to enjoy today."

I nod enthusiastically. "Exactly! Wasn't it you who said 'fuck it and go along with whatever life throws at us'? If we're saying 'fuck it' we might as well make it 'fuck him.'"

Diana laughs. "Oh, you're naughty. I love it!"

I lift one shoulder unapologetically. "Life's too short to worry about shit out of our control. Just enjoy the ride. Pun intended."

We both burst into fits of giggles, falling back into the chairs and clutching our stomachs.

Once our laughter tapers off, I take Diana's hand again. "So glad I met you last night and we got to be roomies."

"Right back at you," Diana says with complete sincerity and squeezes my hand. "Talking about roomies, it feels like all of us have similar stories to how we got invited to ladies' night, yet vastly different reasons for why we're in the Caribbean. I'm curious to hear yours."

I grin at her, but it's bittersweet. "I woke up one morning and realized my life is stuck in the same old pattern. The thought was kind of suffocating, and I knew that if I don't get out now, I'd probably be doing the exact same thing ten years from now, even twenty. So I sold my stuff, packed my bags, and picked a place I've always wanted to visit. I have no real destination or plan in mind. I'll keep going until I run out of money, or I'll get a job somewhere I really like. I met Iris and Helena on the beach about a week after I arrived here. We got to chatting and they told me about the ladies night thing to celebrate Iris's breakup, and invited me to join. They didn't set off any of my stranger-danger senses and it sounded like a good idea since I had nothing else planned. How about you?"

Tucking a piece of her hair behind her ear, Diana looks at the floor as she speaks. "I... um... left home and got on the first flight out from LAX. It just so happened to be coming here."

I sit up straighter and search Diana's face. "Are you okay? Is there someone you're running from?"

Diana's shoulders climb up to her ears. "I might have made it sound worse than it is."

"Girl, don't downplay things with me," I warn her, all defensive instincts on high alert. "If there's someone we need to keep you safe from, you tell me. I'll rally everyone to protect you."

Shoulders relaxing slightly, Diana gives me a soft smile. "I'm okay. The main thing is that I'm safe here and I have no plans on going back."

"If you change your mind and want to tell me more, I'm here for you, okay?" I add earnestly, making sure to meet her eyes so she can see how serious I am.

"Same." Diana shakes her head and switches gears. "Now, since we've established just how cool you are, can I ask you something personal?"

I angle my head and my brows draw together. "Wasn't this whole conversation personal?"

Diana scrunches up her nose and a bright red spreads across her cheeks. "It's about backdoor play. I've always been curious about it. Would you... um... recommend those beads to be a good place to start?"

"Oh, honey. I'm so glad you asked. Embracing your sexuality is the best, most liberating thing you can do for yourself. I'll tell you anything you want to know."

2

Natalie

Diana and I chat until we're called to join the others for breakfast. I give her as many tips and tricks as I can think of, and because we don't have reception on the island due to the magic or something, I promise to send links to some very interestingly shaped toys once we have reception again.

We enter the formal dining room and my eyes jump over all the different figures present, instantly gravitating toward Jasper, only to find his gaze already trained on me. His confident grin tells me he noticed I was looking for him—and he likes it.

That male is a snack. I'd much rather have him for breakfast.

Wordlessly, I saunter toward his side of the room, feeling his eyes like an invisible touch as they track up and down my body. I sway my hips a little more than strictly necessary, letting my short skirt bounce with the movement, hopefully enticing Jasper to glimpse more than he thought he would.

I'm not usually this blatantly obvious about my attraction to someone, but with Jasper, I'm intrigued to a point where I want to push him to his knees, throw my leg over his shoulder, and shove his face in my pussy until I come all over him.

Jasper meets me in the middle of the room and stops an arm's length away.

"Good morning, gorgeous." He leans forward and rolls to the balls of his feet, then rocks back on his heels, tucking his hands in his pockets.

I bite my lip and look at his wavy sandy-blond hair, my fingers itching to sink into the tousled locks around his girthy horns. I mentally bat my lusty thoughts away and settle on a neutral greeting.

"Morning. Sleep well?"

"Would've if I weren't so plagued by inappropriate dreams of a certain woman," the shameless flirt says in his deep timbre.

I trail a hand across my collarbone. "And what would make them inappropriate?" My eyes lock on his warm caramel eyes, and my pussy gets slick at the notion of him having similar thoughts about me.

Jasper's eyes darken. "Perhaps because they weren't just dreams, but things I actually *wish* to do."

"What if this woman likes… 'things'?" I volley back.

Jasper eyes blaze and he brings a fist to his mouth to bite down on. We keep eye contact, silently acknowledging our mutual attraction while the other people in the room mingle and make small talk.

The moment stretches between us like a tightly pulled string and my heart rate ratchets up. Jasper's pulse throbs in his neck and his nostrils flare. For the first time, I see the monster lurking beneath his jovial personality and I swallow against a suddenly dry mouth, all moisture having traveled to my cunt.

The light morning breeze coming in through the open folding doors ruffles my skirt and tickles the backs of my thighs. It's like all my senses are on edge. Just when I think I'm going to have to excuse myself to take care of this building tension, Adelbert clears his throat from somewhere behind me.

"Good morning, ladies and monsters. Please help yourselves to some breakfast," Adelbert says. "We shall discuss our situation once everyone has finished eating."

Jasper and I don't move for a few seconds, blatantly eye fucking each other as the others go about dishing up their food.

The selkie, Erik, interrupts our staring contest with a smile evident in his tone. "Get some food, Jasper. You look hungry. And make sure Natalie gets something to eat too. Your seat is between Everett and Rollo."

Jasper smiles blandly and nods, but doesn't break eye contact with me. The corner of my mouth twitches when I realize neither of us want to leave this little lust bubble we're in.

Finally, Jasper's eyes slide closed and he takes a deep breath in through his nose. When he breathes out again, the fire in his gaze is banked and replaced with determination.

"Let's get you some food, then we can continue... discussing things." Jasper quirks his neck and adjusts his belt, drawing my attention to the substantial outline of his rigid cock tucked into his waistband.

My once-dry mouth waters and I avert my eyes, noticing a few smug smiles on a couple of people pretending not to be staring at us.

"After you," I say and gesture for him to go ahead before I join the ladies on the other side of the room.

Sadie bumps me with her shoulder and fans her face dramatically. "Girl, I swear my own panties were about to catch fire from watching you and Jasper over there."

I lean into her. "You're one to talk. At least you've got all that touching going with Everett."

Sadie smirks and whispers, "Don't tell Adelbert, but I *highly* recommend doing *all* the touching."

I raise my chin. "Noted. I'll see what I can do about that."

At the table, I'm sandwiched between Sadie and Diana on the women's side. Jasper sits slightly across from me, just far enough out of reach that I can't accidentally play footsie with him under the table. I am certain the seating was done with careful consideration on the males' part, because Jamie and Jasper—the known troublemakers—are separated and buffered by calmer personalities.

Once everyone is done eating, Harvey—a minotaur—scoots over to make space for Adelbert to stand at the head of the table. I note Adelbert's grave expression and the tight set to his shoulders. I wonder if all elves are as high-strung as him or if it's the stress of this current situation that exacerbates things. Nevertheless, that male needs to unwind stat.

Conversations quiet down as Adelbert greets us formally. His expression is grave and I fear we're about to get some bad news.

"After extensive research and much deliberation, I have concluded that the information needed pertaining to the marks is not available in this library, and I will therefore need to return to Alberad School for the Supernatural in Germany to scour its more comprehensive resources. The instant I find an answer to a means of dissolving the mark, I shall contact each of you. I hope to do this in an expedited manner so as to not inconvenience you or disrupt your lives any further than you have already experienced. My sincerest apologies for the events thus far."

On our side of the table, the women freeze in their seats and the silence stretches until it's stifling. Clearly, the males already knew what was going to be said because they don't react strongly, only carefully watch our reactions.

Next to me, Diana tries to hide her nerves and I place a comforting hand on her bouncing leg as Adelbert continues talking.

"Due to the distance limit that has come into effect with the marks, I have determined—for the best interest of each individual present—that you shall have to remain with your partner as you leave the island and accompany each other until this matter has been resolved."

Pandemonium breaks loose and a few of the women start talking at the same time, pointing fingers and blaming the males for something they obviously had no say in.

I look up and my eyes automatically fix on Jasper's. There's an apologetic grin on his face and I shrug, nodding in acceptance of what this means. It's clear that no one planned to be magically tattooed and connected to each other with a distance bond.

Raising his voice above the noise, Adelbert interrupts the commotion. "If anyone present can provide a more feasible alternative, I would more than welcome hearing it."

When no one speaks up with any other bright ideas, Adelbert goes around the table and hands each woman his business card so we can contact him if we have any questions or problems.

When he returns to the head of the table, Adelbert says, "For now, I will ask you to speak to your partner. You can decide between yourselves where you will live for the foreseeable future. I cannot yet provide you with a timeline, but I'm leaving today and will start my research tonight. It will be in everyone's best interest to leave as early as convenient, for once I am not present on this estate, I cannot take responsibility for your safety."

On my other side, Sadie looks pale and her sister,

Florence, fidgets with her long blonde hair. Diana's leg starts bouncing again and I gently lay my hand on her thigh and give it a squeeze.

Adelbert draws our attention again and holds up a finger. "Ah, before I forget, the most important element to guarantee your safety. It is imperative that you know that all the males have volunteered to swear an oath of safekeeping to you. Each oath will be tailored to the individual and his species and will be between you, him, and the fates. If you would like a witness, I will be present, or however many other witnesses you desire. At this point, I will ask you to make your way to your partner so you can start discussing your plans."

Without waiting for any more objections, Adelbert beelines for sweet Florence, checking his watch on his way. Everett zooms over to Sadie's seat and I quickly excuse myself to give them more space.

Jasper stands in the doorway leading to the living room and beckons me to follow him. It is like there is some kind of invisible string pulling me to him, because in the next moment I'm on my feet, all too willing to follow him just about anywhere.

3

Jasper

Natalie saunters past me into the living room and I linger in the doorway to watch her plump ass as she heads toward the couch. I plop down next to her, taking care to avoid accidentally brushing against her skin as per the no-touch rule set out by Bertie.

"Looks like you're stuck with me until Bertie can find a way to dissolve the bond," I tell her, trying to keep my gaze on her eyes and not her cherry-red lips with their ever-present tilt that's got trouble written all over it.

I want her brand of trouble.

"Oh no, whatever can we do," Natalie says flatly but the humor in her tone has me perking up. I bite my lip and trail my eyes down her body, noticing how she squirms under my perusal and my cock twitches in response.

Natalie shifts in her seat and leans back, propping her elbows onto the armrest behind her. The move stretches the material of the fitted white T-shirt she's wearing even tighter across her tits. Tits that are begging to be explored with my tongue and teeth.

"Like I said earlier, there are so many things I *wish* to do." I'm only half joking. Natalie has fascinated me since the moment we met and I have not missed the way she's been checking me out. I am oddly self-conscious about my horns and how scary they can seem, but the way Natalie looks at them makes me think she might find them attractive.

"What if I wish for things too?" My heart just about somersaults in my chest at Natalie's words.

"Before you distract me with your wily ways, I need to swear an oath to you. Last night all the guys were in the estate library trying to find ways to dissolve the bonds. When we couldn't find the information we were looking for, we agreed that our main mission is to keep our bonded partners comfortable and make them feel safe. The best way to do so is to swear oaths."

Natalie's brows draw together and she nods. "That's kind of cool of you guys. We all love consent kings. But what about you males? Should we say some kind of oath to you too? You know, since consent goes both ways?"

I lean forward in my seat, getting serious for a minute. "I can't speak for all the males, but I don't need an oath from you. My oath is bound by magic and I'll swear to your safety and comfort. Is there something specific you would like me to add to the wording? Any boundaries you'd prefer to keep?"

Natalie purses her lips and her light eyes flit over my face as she searches for something. She glances toward the dining room where most of the others still mingle in pairs, then drops her voice to a sultry tone just above a whisper. "I like my boundaries to be pushed." Her grin turns sly. "Tell me, how serious are you about this no-physical touch policy?"

I run my tongue along my teeth as I take a second to consider Natalie's question. Despite my very strong desire to play with her and to explore what kind of responses I can draw from her body, there are some bigger elements at play that I need to think about. Crossing the touching line could have consequences and tie us together even stronger than now.

However, *not* touching doesn't seem like something I'd be able to do. And judging by the way she's looking at me, that feeling is very much reciprocated.

"Adelbert is serious about it, only because we do not know the full consequences yet. By laying down that rule, he most likely feels like he's protecting us. I think it's also because elves don't like touch, so it's not exactly a hardship for him. I, on the other hand, love touching. All the touching. So much touching."

Natalie's intake of breath is audible and her pupils expand until only a thin ring of icy blue is visible. It's like my words triggered a shift in the atmosphere as the air grows thick around us. My heart pounds, a throb echoing in my cock, as the rest of the world fades away and I can only see Natalie in front of me.

Natalie shifts again and her little red plaid skirt inches higher, exposing the matching tattoo on the center of her left thigh that matches my tattoo. The urge to trace it is almost visceral.

"So if I asked you to touch me right now?" Natalie's eyes drop to my crotch and the bulge that's impossible to hide. She crosses her legs and her skirt shifts, exposing more creamy skin on lush thighs I can imagine wrapped around my neck.

I clear my throat and pull on my pants to make some room for my lengthening cock. "And how would you like to be touched? I follow directions *very* well."

I'm not sure when it happened, but it's like we're slowly drifting closer to each other with each tension-filled breath we take. Natalie sits up straighter and my arm stretches along the back of the couch. My fingertips tingle with the need to graze her creamy flesh.

"Well, first you can—"

"Don't tell me. Yet." Before I can drag her onto my lap right here, I lean back and lock my fingers behind my head as I slouch into the couch.

I don't usually have a type—it's more based on vibes. And Natalie, she is most definitely a vibe.

But I need to be practical right now. "Let's talk logistics first. We have to decide where we are going to stay while we wait to undo the bond. Do you have any pressing matters to take care of, or any immediate plans you're committed to?"

Not put off by my lack of suave moves, Natalie grins at me. "Nope. I'm free as a bird. Only need to grab my backpack at my hotel, and I don't have a next destination booked yet."

My mind races through the potential outcomes of spending an indefinite amount of time together. Each lascivious look we have shared fuels possible scenarios and I wonder if she's getting as excited as I am.

I try to keep a clear head as I explain, "I kind of have something important to tend to, and it means I will have to take you with me. But of course, if you are uncomfortable, I'm sure he will understand and I can reschedule."

Natalie waves the suggestion away. "Oh no, it's cool. Where we going?"

I slouch deeper and widen my legs. "You wouldn't believe me if I told you."

Natalie tilts her head and her silky black hair sways to the side. "Try me."

Without missing a beat, I say, "The North Pole."

Nodding her head, and with teeth sinking into her full bottom lip, Natalie gives that some thought. "Before meeting you, I would've been skeptical. But you're a krampus. You're the other half of Christmas. So I guess, sign me up. Take me to Santa," Natalie adds, holding her arms wide in invitation.

A boisterous laugh booms from me. Natalie is amazing. She's easygoing, funny, sharp, sexy, and I believe a little bit naughty. Perfection.

When I've got myself under control, I say, "We might bump into Nick, but my plans are actually with his brother, Cole."

Natalie uncrosses her legs and sits up straighter. She twists in her seat to face me more directly, her ice-blue eyes bright with indignation.

Eyebrows raised, she asks incredulously, "Santa has a brother named Cole? Is that just a coincidence or was he named with malicious intent?"

Something warms in my heart at the thought of her already getting defensive on Cole's behalf. Nick's father was cruel to give him that name, but Cole has embraced it and owns it now.

"I'll let him tell you the story," I say and almost reach out to pat her hand in comfort. I catch myself in time, though, and sit back in my seat, mirroring her position.

Natalie's shoulders relax. "Okay. Can't wait to meet him. Just one concern."

"What is it?"

Gesturing down her enticing body, Natalie says, "I don't have anything warm to wear."

My fingers still and I glance down at her outfit. "That cute little skirt of yours is definitely not going to keep you warm." In a low voice filled with appreciation for the sight before me, I add quietly, "It's keeping me very warm, though."

Natalie moves her upper body in a little serpentine dance in her seat. "Oh, you tease. Tell me what else this skirt is doing to you," she says.

"I might have to show you."

"Don't be shy," Natalie purrs.

I clutch my heart dramatically. I think I've finally met my match.

"We're going to have a lot of fun together," I declare, feeling the truth of my words sink into me.

"I'm counting on it."

4

Jasper

Once everyone is done negotiating where they'll spend the coming days as we await the bond's dissolution, we head back to our rooms to gather our belongings. I find Jamie already in the room we shared last night.

Looking up from where he's folding a T-shirt into his bag, my leprechaun friend says, "Wow, lad, you and that Natalie girl sure seemed to hit it off."

I puff up my cheeks and blow out the air as I shake my head. "She's something else. Kind of looking forward to being stuck together."

Grabbing my toothbrush and electric shaver from the en suite bathroom, I can't help but wonder what Cole will say when I show up at his house with Natalie. I know they'll easily hit it off with their dry humor, so I'm sure he won't mind.

I called him earlier to say I'm bringing a woman with me, so he can prepare himself and a spare bedroom for Natalie. He'll also need to request access for her so she can cross the wards into the magical side of the North Pole. He sounded skeptical at first, but I promised him that I'd explain once we get there.

Cole and I have had an interesting relationship over the years. We've never talked about the possibility of things developing into anything serious or permanent between us, especially with him being bound to the Arctic Circle, but the thought has crossed my mind more than once. I've never had the guts to tell him, though. I wouldn't want to burden him with my feelings if he doesn't reciprocate them. It will make working together extremely awkward afterward.

Jamie zips up his bag. His bright green eyes twinkle as he says, "Natalie looks like she's keen on you, too. Unlike my situation with Iris. That woman looks like she's about ready to eat my balls for breakfast." He instinctively cups his balls in a protective motion.

I laugh. "Now that sounds like a great start to the day."

Jamie shakes his head furiously. "Not the way I want it, though. I prefer my balls firmly attached to my body while they're being eaten."

"Fair enough." I clap a hand on his shoulder and ask more seriously, "You going to be okay?"

Jamie presses his lips together and inhales deeply. "Yep. I'll just have to charm her until she can't help but love my sparkling personality."

"Or you could just use all your magic and tricks. That might convince her," I suggest.

Jamie's shoulders deflate and the brightness in his eyes dims a little. "A woman like Iris needs more than fancy tricks to like me."

Grabbing both shoulders, I shake him a little. "You've got lots going for you. Plus, you can fucking teleport."

"Yeah, but no knot. You've got the advantage on me there." Jamie points at my crotch like teleporting isn't cooler than an inflated cock.

I cringe internally and turn back to my bag, adding the last items in. "It's not always the blessing you'd think it would be. Most partners don't quite feel up to taking something like a knot."

Jamie and I are the jokesters of the group. We like to stir the pot and tease and play, but the two of us know what it's like for people to not see beyond that cheerful exterior. After eighteen years of being friends, it's easy to let our guard down around each other and read between the lines.

This time it's Jamie placing a comforting hand on my shoulder. "Ah, lad. Sorry about that. Think Natalie might be up to it?"

"Guess time will tell. But I won't be showing her what I'm packing anytime soon. If she wants to run, it might make things awkward with the distance bond and all."

We grab our bags and head back to the living room to say our goodbyes to everyone leaving for different parts of the world.

Placing my bag at my feet, I lean against the mantle and survey the room. My gaze settles on Natalie where she stands with Diana, Sadie, and Florence—Rollo, Everett, and Bertie's bonded respectively.

An air of excitement has replaced the women's nerves from this morning as more groups huddle around the room, exchanging numbers and hugging each other like they're old friends.

I twist my glamour ring around my finger, and angle my head, feeling the empty air above my head where my horns usually are. It's like a missing limb when I have to hide them, but going out into society with large horns on an otherwise human-looking head is bound to scare people. I love my horns but I hate that aspect about them.

I never take on my full monstrous form, except for when I can't avoid it. But I don't have to worry about Natalie seeing me like that. It's still a long time before the full Krampus Day curse sets in.

Until then, I enjoy my monstrous features only—my horns, knot, and tongue.

Natalie saunters over to me as the couples pair up, readying to leave the island. Being six foot three without my horns, the top of Natalie's head reaches well below my chin. I have to resist the urge to place an arm around her shoulders and drag her against my front. Instead, I keep my hands clasped in front of my body and my focus on Bertie as he tells us about his plans to fix the bonds.

Next to me, Natalie bounces on the balls of her feet and my own excitement has my toes curling in my shoes. I can't wait for her to meet Cole and to see the magic of Joulu.

"Thank you all for your patience and cooperation. Until we meet again," Bertie finishes and gives us all a solemn nod in goodbye. He turns to leave and Florence, taking the no-touch rule very seriously, follows a step or two behind him. The other couples soon head off in their own directions and then Natalie and I are the only two left in the room.

"You ready?" I ask.

"Always," Natalie replies with a wink.

I close my eyes for a second and tell my dick to chill the fuck out. Maybe her answer wasn't meant in a sexual way.

"Back to your hotel to get your stuff?"

Natalie arches a single brow. "Are you asking me or telling me?"

I step in front of Natalie. "Do you like to be told what to do?"

Natalie purses her lips but there's a smile playing around the corners.

"Sometimes," she answers with a challenge in her eyes.

"Oh, Cole is going to love you. He's very bossy. He could tame that brattiness right out of you."

Natalie's expression shifts and her brow furrows. "Oh. You and him?"

"Yeah. But we're not exclusive, it's somewhat undefined. I mean, we're together whenever I'm visiting, but there's no label to our relationship. I don't want to speak on his behalf, but I know him well enough to say that if all three of us are interested, that our time together doesn't have to be boring."

Natalie's eyes burn with a new curiosity and she quirks her head to the side. "I haven't had a multiple-partner situation before, but that might be fun. Depending on if there's any chemistry when we meet. He knows I'm coming, right?"

"Oh, he knows alright. I can promise you there will be chemistry. I won't be surprised if you two tear each other's clothes off within hours of meeting."

"Hours, you say? What if I told you I've wanted to tear *yours* off from pretty much the moment I saw you in that clearing in the jungle?"

"Feeling's mutual, gorgeous. Do you feel like that right now?"

"Yes." Natalie holds my gaze unflinchingly. There's a hunger there that I know is reflecting in my own eyes.

Just as quickly, her brows draw together. "Is this us, or is the magic making us feel like this?"

I tilt my head and draw my lip into my mouth as I ponder that. "I'm not sure. Would it bother you if this was magic?"

After a moment of consideration, the corners of Natalie's lips lift in a smile and she shakes her head. "Honestly, I don't think so. I'm attracted to you regardless."

I study her face, letting my gaze track slowly down to her toes before going back up again, taking in every detail. The way her shirt clings to her tits and the hardened nubs straining for my touch confirm that her body agrees with her mind.

I rub a hand along my stubble and my voice drops into a rumbling purr. "Are you wet for me, gorgeous?"

Natalie squares her shoulders. "Yes."

I take a step closer until she has to tilt her head back to look up at me. "Is your tight little pussy feeling needy?"

"Yes." Her chest heaves up and down with every breath and I can picture how soaked her panties must be.

I shove my hands in my pockets before I can weave my fingers into her hair and slam my mouth against hers. "Do you want to wait until Cole can join us or do you want me to do something about it right now?"

Natalie licks her lips. "I was edging myself all night. I'm so close to coming right now, I think your words might just set me off."

I groan at how sexy Natalie is. The fates might be onto something by letting us cross paths.

Last night, when I burst into the clearing to find the human women standing there, looking nervous and lost, my attention instantly snapped to Natalie and the way I couldn't sense any trepidation from her. Instead, her face filled with curiosity as she surveyed my horns. Since that moment, I've only gotten more intrigued by this beautiful enigma.

"Tell me, darling. How were you edging yourself?" I ask.

A swallow works its way down Natalie's throat, but her gaze never strays from mine. "Anal beads. I wore my string all night." She presses her thighs together as if there's an ache she's dying to sate.

My grin grows and a plan forms in my mind. "And you haven't come since? Do you have them in now?"

"No and no."

"How close are you to your limit? Think you can handle being edged a little longer?"

I appreciate that Natalie takes her time to think about it

before answering. "Going by the traffic light system, I'm not quite at an orange yet, but I'm heading there."

"Do you want to put your beads in again while we travel? I promise I'll take such good care of you when we reach the North Pole."

Natalie's eyes narrow as they flit across my face. Her nose scrunches up as she considers my request. "I'm going to say no on the beads right now. But I'll take you up on the offer to make it good for me once we're there."

Something significant shifts between us and an unidentified emotion settles deep in my gut. "I appreciate your honesty and communicating with me so clearly. I do not take that for granted."

Eyes softening, I get my first glimpse of Natalie's vulnerability beneath all her bravado. I hold out my hand for her, palm up in an open invitation.

"Why delay the inevitable?" I ask, ready to feel her skin against mine.

Natalie sticks out her hand but doesn't quite touch me. "You sure?"

"Very."

"Just don't go catching any feelings, okay?" Natalie says dryly.

I know she's most likely joking, but for *me*, it sure as shit is too late.

5

Cole

My foot taps against the wooden floorboards of my home office as I wait for Jasper and his… companion to arrive. He was vague on the details of *why* he's bringing a human here, but I trust him enough to know there is a reason, and a good one.

Despite his ever-present exuberant disposition and constant jokes, Jasper wouldn't do anything to willingly hurt someone. Nevertheless, I don't know what to expect and that in itself is making me uncomfortable.

I go through the names on my screen and compare them to last year's data, making projections for this coming Christmas. The fact that there even is a Naughty List, and that my father put me in charge of it, still boggles my mind.

Nick, my older half brother, is Santa and gets to make kids happy. My job is to make sure there's enough coal to be stuffed in the stockings of the kids that didn't make the cut. I hate this fucking job, but someone has to do it. Apparently, that someone is me.

The sound of voices outside my house has me looking up from my screen, not like I was actually getting anything done anyway with curiosity bubbling under my skin. I elect not to look out the large window behind me, marching directly for the front door.

Before anyone can knock, I throw the door open, the sleigh bells on my simple teardrop wreath clanking with the movement. My heartbeat quickens as I look for Jasper, for his kind eyes, his curling horns, his bright smile. I've missed him, and my body instinctively leans forward, craving his embrace. But impossibly, all thoughts of my krampus dissolve as I lay eyes on the most stunning creature I've ever seen.

Framed by the tall pines covered in a fresh layer of snow, stands a woman with raven hair and eyes the color of a frozen lake. In them, I can already see us ice skating, not knowing if I'd be able to concentrate on the movement of my feet or getting lost in her eyes that hold more secrets than my own.

I keep my face passive, flicking my eyes to Jasper and the shit-eating grin he's sporting before settling on the woman who spells trouble with a capital T. She assesses me just as blatantly as I do her, her eyes roaming appreciatively over the ink visible beyond the sleeves of my black T-shirt and the holly design on my neck peeking out above my collar. Her full red lips tip up in one corner and there's so much she's saying with that single expression that my cock grows hard instantly.

Out of nowhere, images flood my mind. Images of her on her knees, wrapping those pretty red lips around my cock, infiltrate my mind. Her, begging me to come all over her tits. Her, next to Jasper, both of them bent over the foot of the bed, begging me to fuck them. Them, together as they follow my instructions on what and where to touch. All three of us together and in a hundred different positions.

I blink myself back into the moment, and step forward,

thrusting out my hand for her to shake, "Hey. I'm Cole." I'm surprised how steady my voice comes out and that none of my thoughts have verbalized.

"I've heard so much about you, Cole. I'm Natalie." Her husky voice travels straight through my eardrums and embeds itself somewhere in my brain, ensuring I'll never forget it. Only one other person has ever had such an instantaneous effect on me, and I glance at him as he gives a tiny one-shouldered shrug.

Natalie is drowning in a familiar sweater that can only be Jasper's, the sleeves so long they cover her fingers. She shucks them back—revealing nails painted as black as the T-shirt I'm wearing—and lifts her dainty hand to shake mine.

When her soft skin touches mine, it's like a jolt of heat sears itself from my gut right through every single vessel in my body, leaving a tingling sensation rippling across my skin.

"Did you feel that?" I ask Natalie, not quite ready to let go of her hand yet. A rather odd feeling of wanting to embrace her comes over me, to dip down and smell her hair, to taste her skin. I keep my expression neutral, though, choosing to only raise my brows a fraction as I wait for her answer.

Natalie nods slowly, also making no move to withdraw her hand from mine.

I look to Jasper where he's practically vibrating with excitement.

"Yup," he replies, popping the *p*.

Natalie narrows her eyes at me, then glances over at Jasper. "Um, can we have this conversation inside? It's a little cold out here."

I survey the tiny skirt she's wearing, the tattoos peeking out under its hem, and the bare skin of her thick thighs dotted in goose bumps. Oh fuck, how pretty she would look with my fingers digging into those thighs as she straddles my lap.

"Fuck. Of course. Sorry." I kick the door wider behind me and step back, pulling her in by the hand I'm still gripping. Realizing I might be too intense for her, I let go and gesture to the living room. "Take a seat. Anywhere. There are blankets on the couches. Use those to warm up until I can organize something for you to wear."

Jasper watches Natalie as she makes herself at home and burrows under a fluffy white blanket before he steps up, giving me a sheepish grin. "Hey, Cole."

"You've got some explaining to do." I close the door behind him, ensconcing us in the warmth of the house.

Jasper swallows and I note the traces of stress in the dark circles under his eyes. Underneath the cheery front he puts up for the rest of the world, Jasper feels deeply. It's one of the qualities I admire in him. That, his magnetic smile, and his perky ass.

"Yeah," Jasper says. "I'll tell you everything I can. We don't really know much yet either."

I take Jasper's hand and wiggle the glamour ring off his index finger. He closes his eyes as his horns pop into existence above his head then laces his fingers with mine.

"There. Does that feel better?" I ask as I rub my thumb over the indentation from his ring.

For a fraction of a second, when Jasper opens his eyes, he lets me see beyond the remaining walls that we have both erected between us. My heart accelerates as I try my utmost to keep my emotions from my face, wanting to remain calm in the center of this unknown situation we have found ourselves in.

With my free hand, I put his ring in the melted snowman bowl on the console table, not wanting him to even think about it until he leaves again. Then, aiming to restore a shred of normalcy to our dynamic, I place my hand between his shoulder blades and lightly shove him forward.

"Go make our guest feel welcome."

Before joining them in the living room, I check the thermostat and turn it up a little. Thankfully, the magical realm around the North Pole has regulated the temperature so it doesn't dip too low or heat up according to Earth's fluctuating seasons. Rather, winter remains the only season and a layer of thick snow covers the ground at all times. I keep my house warm enough to be comfortable, but it must be quite an adjustment if they came straight from the Caribbean.

I take a moment to observe Natalie and Jasper from my vantage point in the entryway. They make quite the picture as they sit together on the dark gray couch in front of my bookcase. Each hunter-green hardcover in my collection has been painstakingly rebound by me, the titles foiled in gold along the spines. I find the process of rebinding books to be oddly therapeutic, and the visual just as stimulating.

There's an unbelievable chemistry between Jasper and Natalie, something that mimics my own attraction to both of them. Jasper's body angles toward Natalie, his arm on the back of the couch, hand hovering close to her shoulder as if he's practically restraining himself from reaching for a lock of her hair.

Natalie is much the same. She's kicked off her boots, and her legs are drawn up and tucked under the blanket. Her attention is trained on Jasper as he tells her a story, one hand waving animatedly through the air to emphasize a point he's making. But the way Natalie angles her head as she's listening, tells me she is monitoring me in her peripheral vision.

Good. This means she's very much aware of her surroundings and not some naive woman blindly trusting two monsters. Trust needs to be earned and I intend to show her we're as safe as she wants us to be.

"Has Jasper offered you anything to drink yet? Coffee? Hot chocolate?"

"Not yet. He's been regaling me with tales of mischief you two have gotten up to. But I wouldn't say no to a caffè mocha."

"Whipped cream?"

There's a stretch of silence as my question hangs in the air. Maybe I didn't intend such an outright innuendo, but it's good to test the waters.

Natalie looks me directly in the eyes. "Yes."

I arch a brow at her. "Sweet tooth?"

"I'm afraid so."

Jasper's broad smile is infectious and my own lips quirk up.

Natalie's gaze pinballs between the two of us. "What am I missing?"

Jasper lays a hand on hers, his eyes alight with excitement. "You're in good company, that's all. We love sweet things too. How do you feel about spice?"

"Spice? Like add-a-shot-of-whiskey-to-my-coffee spice? Or spicy food in general?"

"Either or."

Natalie purses her lips and narrows her eyes as she surveys us. Jasper is almost bouncing in his seat as he waits for her answer. I'm scared he's going to tackle her into the couch cushions and lick her from head to toe if she answers in the affirmative. On second thought, that would make a very pretty picture.

Perhaps he could—

"I like some bite to my food. Why?"

"You're perfect." The words fall from Jasper's mouth on a

whispered exhale, his eyes so hopeful it makes my heart ache. I need to get to know Natalie more to make up my own mind, but something deep within me echoes the sentiment.

I don't know what happened on that island or how this stranger ended up on my doorstep, but something tells me I'm in for an adventure.

6

Natalie

"Don't just stand there looking creepy, come sit with us," Jasper says to Cole as he returns with our warm drinks.

Cole sets them on the coffee table in the center of the room. "I made three caffè mochas with gingerbread whipped cream."

Next to me, Jasper sputters out a cough that turns into a chuckle. "Thanks. Just the way you like it."

"Who can say no to gingerbread?" Cole shrugs and gives Jasper a panty-melting wink.

My nipples pebble at the way the two males banter. Even if I don't get their jokes, there's something so hot about their flirting that reflects years of intimacy. Oddly, neither Jasper nor Cole raise any alarm bells for me, which would've been blaring in any other situation. Besides my general jaded outlook on life, I trust these two.

I scoot forward, lifting my mug to my nose so I can take a lungful of the rich aroma. Lowering it to my lips, I take a sip and hum as the flavor hits my tongue.

"This is some good shit," I sigh out as the warm liquid

moves down my throat, my whole body relaxing as I savor the taste. I open my eyes to find both males' gazes trained on me with an intensity I have not experienced before.

Jasper licks his lips. "You like it?"

"What's not to like?"

Jasper whips his head to Cole so fast I'm scared he's going to injure his neck, and Cole's expression can only be described as smug.

I wonder how many secrets these two share.

Cole moves toward the empty armchair on the opposite side of the coffee table. It's framed perfectly in front of the large window that looks out on the quiet forest surrounding his house here on the edge of town.

I still can't believe I'm in the North Pole. It's not so much a pole as a series of villages spread out within the Arctic Circle, carefully warded from human eyes and spelled to retain the same weather all year round. It's magnificent.

Jasper and I entered through a portal on the edge of the central town—where Cole lives—and a literal Christmas elf signed us in. Cole had given our details to their security so we could pass through quickly without too many questions, even though the elves' wide-eyed stares brimmed with curiosity. Apparently, not many humans make their way to this part of the world.

I study the uniquely colored snowcapped trees outside as I sip slowly, savoring the sweet deliciousness of the warm drink.

Pink trees. If someone had told me there were pink trees in the North Pole I would have snorted with laughter. But here I am, looking at the snowy gradients ranging from the palest baby pink on the top layers, to a denser mauve pink where it compacts on the lower branches. It provides the perfect backdrop to the cozy interior of Cole's home, juxtaposing dark and bright.

I can't help but think that it also resembles Cole's and Jasper's energies, one needing the other to enhance their beauty. The rosy glimmer of magic that clings to the snow reflects into the house, bathing the interior in a faint misty pink and I marvel at the beauty of it all. Not in my wildest imagination could I have ever dreamed up this picture.

Jasper tsks. "I hope you're not planning on sitting alone in that chair." The male has an actual pout on his face as he stares at Cole with beguiling puppy eyes blinking exaggeratedly. No one can be immune to those lethal weapons.

A smile creeps across my lips as Cole pauses and cocks his head, studying the two-seater couch that Jasper and I are sitting on, and mentally doing the math.

Jasper adds another flutter of his lashes. "I missed you too much. Please, come sit with us. Natalie doesn't mind. Right, gorgeous?"

Before I can utter my response, Jasper takes my mug and puts it on the table. He places two large hands around my waist and—like it's not the hottest thing that has ever happened to me—lifts me and places me sideways on his lap. I blink while he drapes the blanket around my legs, tucking it in and making sure it's snug before handing me my mug again.

I look at Cole to see his reaction to this, hoping this doesn't cross some line between them, but what I see is not what I expected.

There's appreciation and hunger in those eyes as he eats us up—eyes tracing from where Jasper's hand rests on my waist, up, over the curve of my tits, up the column of my neck, lingering on my lips, before following the same path downward on Jasper.

My pussy grows impossibly wet as the moment suspends between us, the two males having a silent conversation with seriously intense eye contact only.

"I suppose I shall." At Cole's smooth reply, something new flutters low in my stomach.

These aren't nervous flutters. They're anticipation flutters at being on a couch between two ridiculously good-looking males who ooze sex. I could perhaps become the filling in this monster sandwich, and there's nothing on Earth that could make me say no. I don't even have to be the filling, I'd be okay with being a slice of bread. Or the crust. But whatever is happening, I'm in.

Each purposeful step of Cole's feet echoes in my chest as he keeps his eyes on us and moves closer. Holding his mug steady in one hand, he lowers himself down opposite us, gets comfortable, and throws his free arm along the backrest of the couch. Jasper mirrors the move, lacing his fingers with Cole's while his grip on my waist gets a tad firmer.

I take a sip while I mull over the situation more carefully. These two clearly have a deep connection, but they both seem interested in me too. Judging by the horny looks we're all exchanging, I'm counting down the seconds until we get to tear each other's clothes off—just as Jasper promised. Chatting and getting to know each other can come later. After I come. And they come... all over me.

A groove forms between Cole's brows as he looks at us. "Jasper was a little vague on details when he called earlier. How about you two tell me more about how you came to be bonded?" My bottom lip juts out a little in disappointment when I realize Cole's intent on the chatting part first. My pussy will have to wait a little longer to get the attention she craves.

"I'm not sure I understand it myself. Kind of sounded like no one there understood it either—including Bertie," Jasper explains, following Cole's lead and dulling more of my sexy thoughts to focus on the bigger issues at hand.

Cole's eyebrows rise comically high. "Adelbert doesn't know how the bonds came to be either? Or why?"

Out of the corner of my eye, I see Jasper shaking his head. "Not even Bertie. As you know, we were on the Alberad Caribbean Estate for our ten-year school reunion, then despite all the wards erected around the island, a group of human women inadvertently managed to sneak right up to us."

I snicker quietly into my cup at that. He said "erected."

Jasper pinches my waist lightly and playfully nips at my ear, clearly picking up on why I'm giggling, but continues giving Cole more information. "We spent all of last night in the estate library, scouring the books to see if anything can explain why we have to remain within a hundred yards of each other. Now, Bertie has gone back to the Black Forest with Florence—his bonded—trying to look through more comprehensive resources at the main library. He said he'll call us if he finds a way to dissolve the bond."

"And until then you're stuck together?" Cole asks before taking a sip. I unconsciously copy the move, enjoying the balance of sweetness with a slight kick of ginger as the warm liquid passes my lips, having zero sexy thoughts about other warm liquids that can pass my lips.

"Yup. I swore to keep Natalie safe as long as she's with me. Initially, Bertie told us not to touch until we got answers."

"Let me guess, the two of you found that a little... hard?" Cole snorts and I giggle along with him. He's not wrong.

"Natalie said she doesn't mind touching." Jasper squeezes my waist, emphasizing his statement, and I lean a little further into him.

"Did she now?" Cole's question sounds like it's aimed at Jasper, but his eyes stay firmly fixed on me.

I lift my chin a little and stare right back at Cole. "Yes, she did."

I study his sharply pointed ears and the multiple piercings decorating it, his septum piercing I didn't know I'd find attractive but suddenly really admire, then the tattoos starting at his throat, moving down his arms and covering almost every visible piece of skin up to his wrists. I wonder how far down his body they go.

"Are you comfortable there, Natalie?" Oh fuck, the way my name sounds when Cole says it has me squirming on Jasper's lap, trying to squeeze away the pulse drumming in my clit.

Jasper snakes his hand higher and splays it over my stomach, the material of the sweater bunching under his wide palm. Placing his mouth next to my ear, his breath is hot against my skin as he chastises me in a low voice. "Naughty, naughty, Natalie. You can't go squirming on my lap like that if you don't want to wake the beast."

I let out an embarrassing cackle. "The beast? Seriously?" I look to Cole to see if he's reflecting my sentiment, but I only get the arch of a brow back.

"Keep squirming like that and you'll find out," Cole says. I pause and look over my shoulder at Jasper. The confident grin he gives me confirms he wasn't really joking. It kind of makes me want to grind down and find out if he really is as big as I thought I imagined on the island.

"You still cold, Natalie?" Cole asks, gaze dipping down to my tits where my nipples are trying to punch holes through my bra.

I arch my back a little and watch as his throat works on a swallow. "I'm good, just my fucking feet that are cold. Trudging through snow in boots that aren't really waterproof has turned my toes into little icicles."

"Would you mind if I warmed them for you?"

"Oh, you don't have to do that."

"I believe I asked if you minded if I did that. I'm perfectly capable of making my own choice in this regard."

I bite my lip as my pussy basically gushes at his words. Bossy Cole is hot.

"Sure," I answer in a voice smaller than I'm used to, my heart beating faster than the wings on a tiny creature. I'm usually the one taking control in situations, but Cole telling me what to do, and me following very willingly, is a whole new ball game. One I'm cautiously welcoming.

"Now you just get comfortable and lean back against Jasper while I take care of your feet. Sound good?"

My head nods of its own accord and I automatically sink into Jasper's embrace.

When did I become so pliant? And with practical strangers?

Jasper hugs me closer to him and slips a digit under my sweater, trailing it lightly across my skin. Seeing no protests from me, he works his whole hand under my sweater and caresses my skin in gentle circles while Cole tracks each move and studies our faces. I cling to my mug like it's the only thing still making sense in this version of heaven I'm currently in.

Seemingly satisfied that we're staying put, Cole untangles his fingers from Jasper's and places his mug on the table. Jasper uses his now-free hand and brushes my hair behind my ear before putting it under the blanket and resting it on my thigh. His touch seers my skin and my panties get damper with every second that passes. I don't know how much more I can take before I'll be dripping down my thighs.

Eyes fixed on me, Cole slowly folds the blanket back and gently lifts my feet into his lap. Jasper keeps up his sweet torturous caresses against my skin, tracing soothing patterns against my thigh with one hand, and with his other, slips his pinky underneath the band of my skirt. My breath stutters at the tenderness of the moment.

Sex, I can do. Fun. A good, fast fucking is what I like. Gentle caresses and sweet gestures are what I have trouble with, because they usually spell out feelings. But I've only just met these two and all three of us have insane chemistry. This is just leading to fucking, right?

Sensing my apprehension, Cole pauses his movements and looks at me with poorly disguised concern. "You okay there, Natalie?"

Jasper pauses too and leans around me to look at my face. "I know you said you liked your boundaries pushed, but if this is too much it all stops right now. No hard feelings."

I look from one male to the other. Hard lines and soft. Short and tall. Dark and light. Yin and yang. Both patiently waiting for me to decide if I want to keep going.

I purposefully grind against Jasper, then wiggle my toes at Cole. Using my most sultry tone, I say, "Don't stop now."

Jasper lowers his forehead against my shoulder and a groan vibrates from somewhere deep inside him. "You heard the lady, Cole." Skimming his lips against my ear, Jasper whispers, "I'm very well acquainted with Cole's fingers. They're magical. Wait until you see what else he's hiding."

I raise my eyebrows at Cole but he only smirks back as he pulls off both my socks. He starts massaging one foot, warm fingers digging into the arch, and a satisfied moan crawls up my throat and lands in the air between us.

My mug wobbles in my hand as sensations war through my body. Jasper, keeping a careful watch of all my reactions, notices and leans forward to take the cup from me and place it on the table—all while holding me firmly in his lap. When he sits back again, his hand is higher on my inner thigh than before, and I subtly part my legs to give him better access.

The only negative thing about my thick thighs is that it's

less easy for a hand to slip between them. On the other hand, they do make fantastic ear muffs—something I hope to prove to these males soon.

Underneath me, I feel the stirrings of a hardening cock and another breathy moan escapes from me when Cole blows warm air over my icy toes. I don't know when I closed my eyes, but they fly open when Cole switches feet and repeats the same actions.

At this point, I know I'm dripping through my panties and even possibly onto Jasper's pants. All of my own edging yesterday is culminating with these four hands on me right now.

Slowly, I start rocking my hips in tiny circular motions, grinding down on the incredibly hard cock underneath me. Jasper's fingers dig into my skin as he wordlessly pulls me closer.

Dragging his nose up my neck, Jasper sends goose bumps skittering across my skin. "Feeling a little needy, Natalie?"

"You know I am." I try to make my voice sound snappy, but my whimper following the last word gives away just how horny I am.

Cole tuts. "Can't have that now, can we? I don't want our guest to feel dissatisfied at any time. Want to tell us what you need, Natalie?"

"More," I pant.

Jasper's hands still on me as he gets some kind of signal from Cole. I try to squirm against him again, but those hands are strong and hold me firmly in place.

"Let's try that again. Use your words, Natalie. Tell us exactly what you want."

"Touch me. Please. I need to come. So bad."

Seemingly on my side, Jasper adds, "Our darling Natalie was edging herself for a long time before we got here. I think we should help her out."

All serious, Cole asks, "Are you aching, Natalie?"

"Yes."

"Are you wet?"

"Yes."

"Can you show us how much?"

I nod.

"Words, Natalie. We need your words."

"Check for yourselves," I sass back.

"Jasper, can you help spread those beautiful thighs for us?"

"It will be my pleasure."

Jasper throws the blanket off me and repositions me so that my back presses to his front, draping each of my legs over his thighs. He laces his fingers with mine, then bands his arms across my torso, rendering me immobile. Slowly, he widens his legs until mine are spread obscenely and my soaked underwear can no longer be hidden.

I don't think I have been this turned on in my life.

The sound of two males simultaneously scenting the air, has my pussy clenching around nothing.

"Mmm, doesn't she smell good, Jas?"

"So sweet. I bet she tastes even better."

"Want to find out?" I pipe up, needing someone to touch me before I do it myself.

"You could ask nicely, Natalie. Ask Jasper to stick his fingers in that sweet cunt of yours so I can lick them clean. I want to see if you taste as good as you smell."

Holy fuck. A shiver races down my spine at Cole's filthy words and I arch instinctively against Jasper, grinding against the thick cock lodged against my ass.

"Please," I breathe, incapable of more eloquent requests.

Jasper, being the merciful male that he is, lets go of my hands, patting me in a motion to let me know I'm not to move my arms. His hands skate down the outside of my legs before turning back, repeating the motion on the inside of my thighs. I watch as he skims over my tattoo band that circles my upper thigh, the tattoo we share almost blending seamlessly with its design.

My heart hammers inside my chest, but I know I'm not alone. Behind me, Jasper's chest rises and falls in tandem with mine, and on the other side of the couch, Cole stares at us like it's Christmas and we're his shiny new toys.

"Oh, darling," Jasper groans as his fingers meet some of the moisture that has made its way through my panties and onto my inner thighs. His fingers move over my tiny black thong and traces the seam of my pussy.

"Cole, these panties are ruined for us. They're absolutely soaked through."

"Better to take them off then. Natalie only deserves the best. Here, let me help."

I look up as Cole comes to stand in front of us, focusing on my parted lips before meeting my eyes again. Silently, I nod at him, giving him permission to do whatever he wants with my body.

Cole sinks to his knees between my spread thighs and hooks his fingers in the sides of my thong, gently maneuvering it down my legs.

My breath hitches and a hot, reckless flutter takes flight deep in my stomach as Cole's gaze zeroes in on Jasper's finger spearing my soaked core. Jasper pulls it out and adds a second finger, pumping it in and out, as I mewl with need. The obscene sloppy sounds of my arousal fill the room, accompanied by my panting and the labored breathing coming from the males.

Hands still resting on my spread knees, Cole tells Jasper, "Taste her."

Fuck, fuck, fuck. This is so hot. I think I've died and gone to heaven.

Jasper brings his fingers to his mouth and I move my head to the side to watch as he sucks them clean. His eyes roll back in his head and a moan rumbles out of him like it's the best thing he's ever tasted.

"Sugar cookies," Jasper says breathily with a dopey grin adoring his face.

"What?" I ask, unsure if I heard him correctly.

"Let me taste," Cole demands.

Doing something unexpected, Cole stands up and leans over me to kiss Jasper. He collars the much larger male, fingers digging into Jasper's jaw as he holds his head still to devour his mouth. My pussy must be dripping onto the floor at this rate. This is just getting hotter and hotter.

As they kiss, Jasper's fingers return to my cunt and pump in and out while grinding his palm against my clit.

Cole breaks the kiss and looks at me, lips wet and swollen from their hungry kisses. "Sugar cookies," he confirms.

Then, he leans down and claims my mouth in a bruising kiss. There's nothing shy or tentative about it. He plunges his tongue into my mouth, and I try to meet him stroke for stroke while my pussy tightens around Jasper's fingers, now crooked inside of me and rubbing against the perfect spot. Cole's fingers weave into my hair and he angles my head just where he wants me, demanding I surrender to him—to them. I grip Jasper's arm while I fist Cole's T-shirt with the other hand, drawing them both closer to me, wanting more and more and more.

With one hand still around Jasper's throat, Cole speaks against my lips, but his words are for Jasper, "Make her come while I swallow her screams."

"Yes, sir," Jasper says. He instantly adds a third finger and I relish the stretch, rocking my hips into his hand as he plays my body like it's his own.

Cole licks against my mouth and I open for him, and

together our tongues duel in an ancient dance that was choreographed just for them. He swallows all my whimpers, my moans, and I feel myself giving more to these two males than just my pleasure.

My orgasm builds low in my spine, and my thighs tremble. Sensations light my veins on fire as the males drive me close to the edge.

"Come for us, Natalie. Now," Cole demands, and his words shove me right over.

My eyes close and my breath is robbed from me as my orgasm crashes through my body like a ten-foot wave. My pussy squeezes around Jasper's fingers, a gush of liquid following, and I scream. Cole takes all my sounds into his mouth as the two of them let me ride it out.

Slowly, they guide me back to the present, gently letting me settle into this realm where I just had my first taste of a threesome with two of the most handsome males I've ever met.

I'm in trouble, because nothing could possibly be as hot as this ever again.

7

Jasper

"*H*as someone seen my panties?" Natalie asks, strutting into the kitchen after a trip to the bathroom to—unfortunately—clean up the delicious evidence of her release.

My hands pause from stirring the soup on the stove, and I give her bare legs a longing look. "What do you need them for? Won't they just get in the way?"

Oh, to be trapped between those thighs while I eat my fill...

"Har har." Natalie walks right up to me and places a finger under my chin to bring my eyes to meet hers. "I want to wash them. If you haven't noticed, I have a limited supply of clothes."

"About that." With a loud thud, Cole places a box on the kitchen table. "I ordered some things for you while I was making our drinks earlier. You're going to need warmer clothes and a coat if you're staying for a while."

Natalie quirks her head at the rather sizable box. In the rest of the world, delivery boxes are plain, but true to the Christmassy nature of this place, this one is a festive red and has a ribbon attached to the top. It kind of matches the deep red door handles on the dark oak cabinets of the kitchen.

"That was fast. Magically fast? And unexpected, but thank you. How long do you think I'm staying for?"

I place two fingers on her forehead and smooth out her frown. "Haven't heard anything from Bertie yet. So it could be a few days, maybe even weeks?"

Cole leans a shoulder against the wall and looks at Natalie. "Do you have somewhere to be?"

"Not really. I sold all my stuff in Arizona before I left for the Caribbean. That backpack with me is everything I own."

"And now this box too," he says. Thankfully, things move really fast up here, so Natalie didn't have to go long without proper warm clothing.

Natalie shakes her head. "I'll return everything when I leave."

I stand up straighter as my brain finally registers what she said. "Hold on. Sold everything? Where are you going?"

Raking a hand through her hair, Natalie licks her lips before she speaks. "I didn't really have a destination in mind. I needed to get away. To start over."

Cole and I both go on alert at the same time, sharing a look as our spines stiffen, ready to battle whatever or whoever has caused Natalie trouble.

In a tone brokering no argument, Cole demands to know, "Why?"

Scrunching up her nose in the cutest way, Natalie sighs, "Are we doing the deep bonding moment thing now?"

Cole moves in front of Natalie. "We sure are." He places a quick, fierce kiss on her lips and, before she comes out of her dazed state, takes her hand and leads her to the kitchen table. My cock stirs at the sight and how right it feels with the three of us together. There was a beautiful harmony earlier on the couch, something that just worked, and I'm excited to see where things could lead later tonight.

Sinking down into a chair, Natalie holds up a finger, pointing first to Cole, then at me, then wagging it in the space between us. "If I share, you have to share. I need more info about what's going on here."

I smirk. "You mean, you want to know more about us, besides what my fingers feel like in your tight cunt or Cole's tongue in your mouth?"

Natalie blows out a breath and throws her hands dramatically in the air. "And this is why I need my panties. Keep saying things like that and I'll be dripping all over the floor."

I wiggle my eyebrows. "Then I'll gladly follow behind and lick it up."

"Jasper," Cole chides but there's laughter sitting right beneath the surface.

Raising a hand to mock salute him, I say, "Let's eat and share, then we can do fingers-and-tongues chats after."

Natalie taps a black nail against the tabletop. "And cocks. I didn't miss the fact that neither of you got to come. I'm all about equal opportunity and leaving my partners satisfied."

My smile grows wolfish, knowing she's unaware of why we stopped after only focusing on her pleasure. "Oh, you'll have to work up to our cocks."

Scoffing, Natalie says, "Listen, I'm not some inexperienced woman. A cock is a cock."

Cole shakes his head. "Not with us, it's not."

"Huh?"

I bite my lip, relishing the look of almost innocent bafflement replacing Natalie's usual self-assuredness. "I doubt you've seen anything like either of us have."

Placing both hands flat on the table, Natalie's wide-eyed gaze swivels between Cole and me. Excitement and disbelief war in her tone, as she asks, "Are monster cocks real?"

"Yup." My chest puffs up with pride and I cross my arms, confidence running through my veins that Natalie was made for us.

Cole clears his throat and adjusts his dick under the table. "Let's keep on topic before said monster cock drills a hole through my pants."

Natalie shakes her head like she's willing her lustful thoughts away as she arranges a throw blanket over her lap, unfortunately covering those delectable thighs.

"Okay, okay. I'll tell you whatever you want to know—as long as everyone's sharing. But don't think your monster cocks aren't on the forefront of my brain. I'll probably be distracted coming up with all sorts of theories about monster cocks while we try to have this conversation."

"Noted. Now, Arizona?" Cole asks and sits back in his chair, manspreading his legs in a way that makes me think of our countless nights together of me sitting between them as he strokes my hair.

"I'm twenty-five and was working as a receptionist in a tattoo studio, getting ready to start my apprenticeship, and then I guess I had an existential crisis." Natalie's tone is flat, but there's a bit of humor lurking underneath.

"Well, the North Pole is a great place to ponder your life," I say. I know it sounds like a joke, but I really love visiting here more so than staying at my own place.

A corner of Natalie's lips quirk up. "You sound like you're talking from experience."

I just shrug like it's not a big deal, and feel Cole's gaze burning the side of my face.

Natalie takes a fortifying breath before elaborating. "Things weren't always easy growing up. I was raised by a single mom who worked a lot to make ends meet, you know the drill. Once I was old enough to support myself, I moved out to lessen her burden. From pretty early on in life I knew

I didn't want to follow in her footsteps—especially the pregnancy stuff, I'm annoyingly meticulous about my birth control. But somehow I found myself with a job that made enough to sustain me, but not enough to give me the opportunities to really live the life I want for myself. I realized one day that I was going to be stuck in Arizona my whole life, same as her, and never go on adventures or see the world. So I sold everything, packed a bag, and left. I have no final destination in mind, just an itch to get out and the knowledge that I don't want to go back there."

"You're welcome to stay here as long as you want," Cole says. "I'm sure we can think up an adventure or two for you." The offer is sweet, but there's something heady underneath it, like a promise that he might actually give her a reason to extend her stay.

I hope we can both stay.

Like most krampuses, I have a modest cabin nestled in the Alps, but I find myself spending increasingly longer periods of time at Cole's house, feeling more at home here than when I'm alone there. Things between us have even gone so far that I've upgraded from having a drawer in his room, to my own closet space. Yet, we've never had *that* conversation to label our relationship.

Natalie's smile is faint, but genuine, before she settles for her usual impassive expression. "I go where Jasper goes, I guess, for however long this tattoo is keeping us tied to each other."

"Can I see the tattoo?"

"Oh, I thought you saw it. It's here." The spoon in my hand falls still, the soup bubbling softly as I watch her remove the blanket around her waist and point to the design that blends into the garter belt of flowers tattooed in a ring around her upper thigh. Unconsciously, I rub the same spot on my leg.

Cole moves around the table and traces the aligned sun, moon, and stars. His touch sends a visible tremor racing through Natalie. When she looks up again, Cole's dark eyes are firmly locked on hers. My own breathing gets shallow as an awareness builds between them before Cole pries his hand away and slumps back into his chair.

"You can trace mine too," I say, releasing the spoon, letting it clatter against the edge of the pot while I reach for my belt buckle.

"Fuck, Jas. If you take your pants off now then this conversation is done for. My hands will be wrapped around your knot before you can blink and Natalie will be swallowing your delicious cum like the good girl I know she is."

I groan and fist my hard cock through my pants. "You can't go putting an image like that in my mind right now. How am I supposed to concentrate on stirring this soup?"

"I agree," Natalie says and crosses her legs. One elbow on the table, she props her chin in her hand. "Knot? And delicious cum? You've piqued my interest."

"You two horny creatures," Cole tuts with mock disapproval. "Let's focus on the conversation."

"You started it." I pout, but partially turn back to the soup while keeping them in my peripheral vision.

Cole sighs. "Wouldn't have if you two didn't look so tempting."

Natalie likes to pretend that she's unaffected, but the rosy color blooming on her cheeks is giving away just how much she likes the banter between us three and the irresistible draw we have to each other.

Taking a deep breath, I prepare myself for my turn to share. Natalie opened up and told us about things I'm guessing she doesn't share easily, so it's only fair that I meet her vulnerability with my own.

"Okay, back story. I'm twenty-eight, Cole is thirty.

Together, we work on Santa's Naughty List. Around the middle of the year, Cole's brother Nick gives him a list of names and it's up to Cole to ensure there is enough, well, coal to go into each stocking. I take the names of the naughtiest kids, and around Krampus Day it's my 'job' to scare them into being good."

"Scare them?" Natalie asks, completely flabbergasted. "Jasper, you're the least scary thing I've ever seen. If possible, I'd even go so far as to say you're sunshine. You're cute, kind, funny. No way anyone would find you scary. Also, that sounds like a pretty crap way to spend Christmas."

I swallow hard and tuck my hair behind my ear. "You don't think the horns are scary?"

"The horns are hot," Natalie states succinctly, like there was ever any question of them being anything but.

Heart hammering like it's trying to fight its way out of my chest cavity, I say softly, "There's something else too…"

Natalie sits up straight, turning her whole body to face me. "You don't owe me anything, Jasper. Don't tell me stuff you're not comfortable with sharing."

"Natalie's right, Jas. You can tell her later," Cole says gently.

I shake my head. "No, it's fine. She won't see me like that." I look at Natalie, trying and failing to keep the insecurity from my voice as I say, "I don't want anyone to see me like that." I drag in a slow breath and gather my courage to tell her my deep secret. "Being a krampus means I'm cursed in a way. You know how werewolves transform with the full moon? In a similar sense, a krampus who chooses not to live in their fully shifted form, transforms into their natural state around Krampus Day. For the first week of December, I'm bound to my monster form, and not the semishifted state that I usually am in—like now. I lose a hold of my, for lack of a better word, humanity."

"Sounds hot to me," Natalie says with a shrug.

My head rears back. "It's not. I'm ugly. And dangerous. Scary. I hate that part of my life and I usually lock myself away so I don't succumb to my instincts to chase people—or gods forbid children—through the streets. December should be a happy time, filled with excitement for Christmas and presents, and making memories. Not being scared."

"Seriously, I'd be happy to be locked up with you. You can chase me anytime," Natalie says and winks at me. I don't think she truly understands how scary a krampus can look, so I let her comment slide and chalk it up to her just trying to be nice.

I decide to give her a bit more backstory since she was forthcoming about her family. "My parents are still happily mated and live together in a fancy cabin in the Alps, only one mountain over from my place. They hate wearing glamour rings and prefer to remain in their natural krampus forms. They're not as sensitive to their instincts since they isolate themselves and chase each other instead—something a kid shouldn't think about their parents doing. I like to go visit them when I can, but I don't like being reminded of what I actually look like."

Not waiting for any comments from them and needing to divert the focus from me, I say to Cole, "Your turn."

Cole takes the hint and saves me by revealing his vulnerability. "I'm Santa's secret second son, and his biggest regret."

Natalie's eyes widen until the icy blue of her irises look like little snowflakes in her big eyes. "Excuse me? What the fuck? I thought Santa is supposed to be nice."

Running a hand over his shortly shorn hair, Cole explains, "My father is retired now, and in his own way, he has tried to be nice over the years. But his grief has tainted his life. Nick, my older half brother and current Santa, took over the job much younger than is customary. Long story short, Santas have historically only had one child—a son. They're all named Nick. But after the unexpected death of his wife, my father spent one night with my mom, a Christmas elf, and I was the very unexpected result."

"Holy fuck. That must've been so hard," Natalie says and places a hand on top of Cole's.

I know this story so well, yet every time I think about it, anger and hurt on Cole's behalf roil deep within me. I've wanted to speak up and tell his family how much he hates his job, about the labels put on him by the other elves, but he never wants me to step in. Says he'll handle it himself, though he has yet to say anything to them.

Cole turns his hand over and squeezes Natalie's. "It's not been easy. Because of my Christmas-elf side, I'm bound to remain within the Arctic Circle, unless accompanying Santa on Christmas business—something I have never done before. I'm not really welcomed by the other elves since I'm seen as bad luck. Elves basically worship Santa, and he didn't want me, so…"

"Where is Daddy Santa now?" Venom drips from Natalie's words like she's about to go out and search for him herself, ready to seek vengeance for Cole.

"In a cabin somewhere, wallowing his life away," Cole answers with a grimace. "My brother works really hard to keep up Christmas cheer, making up for the gap my father has left. Despite being in his late thirties already, he hasn't taken a wife yet, something very odd for Santas who usually get married quite young."

"Do you hate your father?" Natalie's straightforward question causes Cole to pause, thinking it over before he answers.

"No. I think grief can make people act out of character, they make mistakes. I know I was an accident and he regrets that I'm the walking embodiment of his moral failure when he still felt loyal to his wife, but my mere existence is a painful reminder of it all."

"You're really nice. Much nicer than I could ever be. I would've been bitter," Natalie says with her mouth turned down and righteous fire burning in her eyes on Cole's behalf. "Where's your mom?"

"She lives in one of the toy-making villages. Last I heard, she got married." Cole shrugs like it's no big deal, but I know how hurt he was by his mom not inviting him to the wedding. She tried making some feeble excuse about the other elves maybe being uncomfortable with his presence. Thankfully, Cole didn't fall for her lines and he ceased all contact with her right then.

Needing Natalie to understand how good Cole really is, I add, "This is also why Cole lives on the edge of town. He's giving the Christmas elves space."

Cole shrugs again but there's a hint of pain in his eyes before he glances away and stares out the window. "I like my space, and if it can help the others be more comfortable, then so be it."

"Isn't it lonely?"

Natalie's question has me holding my breath. I've always wanted more with Cole, but toward the end of every stay there comes a time when he pushes me away, saying a life with him bound to the Arctic wouldn't be fair. I've wondered if he was embarrassed of me, or the way the elves fear me bothered him, but I think it's because he thinks *he* won't be enough for me.

"It's fine," Cole says and there's a finality in his tone that indicates this conversation is done for now.

"Who's hungry?" I ask, wanting to shift the focus away from Cole and onto something else.

Natalie picks up on what I'm trying to do, and gives me a

lascivious once-over, gaze lingering below my belt. "I can think of something I'd like to eat."

"Food first, then we can get back to talking about cocks and where we're going to put them," I say with a wink.

"Soon." I don't know if that single word from her is a request or a demand, either way, I'm in.

Cole

After dinner, I light the fire in the hearth and we all get cozy with hot chocolate and floating marshmallows. This time, Natalie takes the wide armchair and curls up by herself under the blanket she has now commandeered as her own.

I revel in the quiet moment, soaking up the presence of two other people in my home at the same time, the crackle of the logs and soft rustle of clothing being the only sounds in the room. There's something so right, so special about this moment, about them—I just can't name it yet.

With dimmed lights throughout the house, I'm entranced by the way the light and shadows from the fire dance across Natalie's features, highlighting her high cheekbones and full lips as she stares hypnotized at the flames.

Behind her, magical pink flakes land delicately on the tall trees surrounding my property, dampening any other sounds that might come from the town. I've always loved snow and I long to play with it the way Nick can, but the Santa magic to control the weather has never manifested in me.

"Natalie, have you ever had sugar plums before?" Jasper

asks with a smirk in his voice, punctuating the comfortable silence. I almost do a spit take, but disguise my surprise with a cough.

Eyes flitting between Jasper and myself, Natalie looks skeptical. "That's random. What am I missing?"

My "nothing" is drowned out by Jasper's "sugar plums are delicious."

I shake my head and playfully flick him with a finger against his shoulder. "Not cool, Jas. This was a peaceful moment and you're trying to sex it up."

"I was not," Jasper says with a faux sulk that I don't buy for one minute. "I was merely asking her about Christmas-themed food."

"Sure, you were." Natalie's skepticism is ripe in her tone.

I place my hand on Jasper's knee. "Jas, the fake eyelash-batting thing you're trying isn't working on either of us. I know Natalie has only known you for a few days, but she can already read you like a book too." My half smile gives away how endearing I find his act, despite my attempt at calling him out.

Natalie nods. "Sorry to say that's true. It's cute, though. Bat away, but they're not distracting me from what you said. Explain, please."

Jasper leans back and spreads his legs. Mischief colors the air around him and I brace myself for what he's going to reveal about me.

"Cole's cum tastes like sugar plums and I hope you like the flavor, because you'll never taste anything better."

Calmly, Natalie places her empty cup on the coffee table before sitting back again, crossing her arms across her chest. "Forgive me if I misheard that, but did you just say that Cole's cum tastes like sugar plums?"

Jasper draws his lower lip between his teeth and nods slowly. Sitting forward, he wiggles his eyebrows. "It's so good. I want to drink him down all day. Same as you. I can get addicted to your cunt."

There's a faint stain of red across Natalie's cheeks and the tiny smile she's trying to contain gives away just how much she likes what Jasper's saying. Hearing him talk about me so openly, so proudly feels like tiny snowballs are being pelted around in my stomach. And Natalie's interest in him, in me, in us three *together*, it sparks a whole new emotion I have yet to name. But it feels like… potential.

"Interesting," Natalie nearly purrs. "And tell me, Jasper, what does your cum taste like?"

Before he can tell her, I silence him with an arched brow. He slumps into the couch and pushes his bottom lip out. If we want Natalie to like us, we can't info dump on her when she just got here. Despite what we've already done together, I want to take it as slow as our bodies will allow.

Wanting to avoid any misunderstandings about why I stopped the conversation there, I explain, "We don't want to overwhelm you with a ton of things on the first day. If you only found out monsters were real days ago, I'm sure your mind is spinning. Let's maybe get some rest and reconvene in the morning. And if you're still curious in the light of day, you decide for yourself what it tastes like."

Combing her hair back with her fingers, Natalie looks between the two of us, then nods. "I can't believe I'm saying this, but that might be a good idea. Don't go thinking I forgot that you said you had monster cocks too. I want to see them so bad. But knowing that you come with flavors, I might just have my mouth stuck to you day and night."

Smirking, I drawl, "If that's what you want, I won't stop you."

Jasper sits up again, eyes shining brightly. "Maybe before bed we can—"

I shake my head. "Not happening. You're exhausted. You

didn't sleep much yesterday with all the research. Let's chat in the morning."

Jasper pouts and I squeeze his cheeks between my fingers to push his lips out even more. Mumbling through his squished mouth, he asks, "What time are you leaving for work?"

My brows rise high and my hand drops to my lap when I realize I haven't even thought about work since Jasper and Natalie crossed my threshold. I haven't missed a day of work in my life, but I can think of nothing worse than being stuck in front of my computer or in virtual meetings while Jasper and Natalie are at home—without me.

Not believing the words until they're out of my mouth, I say, "I'm calling in sick tomorrow."

KNOCK. Knock.

Who the fuck could be knocking on my door? I never get visitors, Jasper basically being the only one, and he's currently singing in the shower.

"Can someone get the door, please?" I call, not wanting to leave my spot at the stove and risk burning our breakfast.

"I've got it," Natalie answers. It's strange how seamlessly Natalie has fit into my house. There's an easiness between us, besides the explosive chemistry, that makes it feel like she's been here for months.

Last night, I gave her the spare bedroom, feeling like she might need the space to acclimate to this new world she's found herself in. I spooned Jasper through the night, letting my hand graze his cock while whispering sweet fantasies into his ear about the three of us, but not allowing him—or myself—to come.

Today, I'm spun so tight my cock has been in a constant state of arousal, and I'm sure Jasper is in the same delicious state. But we both decided to save our cum for Natalie. When she told us she wanted to see, to *taste*, I knew I wanted to give it all to her. I want to watch her suck me dry as Jasper paints her face with his cum.

"Um, Santa's here," Natalie says, her tone weary but cheerful as she steps into the kitchen.

"Morning, Cole." I turn when I hear Nick's rumbly voice. My spatula clatters to the floor when I see him standing there with a big pot in his mittened hands. Next to him Natalie' eyes are nearly bugging out of her head as she surreptitiously points to Nick and mouths excitedly, "Santa."

My brain short-circuits for a moment as the two of them look like opposite sides of a coin. Natalie is so sexy in her new tight black shirt and leggings, and Nick is wearing the funniest red sweater with literal blinking Christmas lights adorning a tree—probably sent as a gift from a human who doesn't even know that Santa is real.

Quickly picking the spatula up again, I can't hide the surprise from my voice as I greet my half brother. "Hey. What you doing here?"

The bear of a male's eyebrows furrow as he explains hesitantly, "You called in sick. You're never sick. So I brought you some chicken soup."

"Fuck." The word is a little more than an exhale. I didn't see his concern coming.

Nick looks around the kitchen, pausing on the stack of pancakes already cooked before back at me. "But, perhaps you're not sick?"

My heart nearly sinks to the soles of my feet. "Um... No."

"Morning," Jasper singsongs as he practically bounces into the kitchen. "Oh." He pauses and his eyes flick between me and Nick, then Natalie, before going back to Nick again.

"Morning, Nick. Wasn't expecting you," he says brightly, ignoring the awkwardness in the room.

"Yeah. I'll just go. Sorry for interrupting you guys. Here's the soup. You can warm it on the stove and—"

"Nick. Sorry, I can explain. Please stay. Join us for breakfast."

"Oh, I don't want to intrude."

"No, really. There's more than enough. Plus soup. Have a seat," I insist, feeling guilty for having lied to him about being sick, and owing him an explanation at least.

"Come on, Santa. I'm guessing you don't have breakfast with a krampus, a human, and your half brother every day," Natalie cajoles, sweeping a hand through the air to take us all in.

"And what do you know, there are enough seats. Take this one." Jasper pulls out the chair closest to Nick and gives him a look that instantly has him putting down the pot before carefully lowering his large frame onto the wooden chair.

"Oh, thank you," Nick says nervously but with genuine appreciation shining in his eyes. I've been so caught up in my own life that I haven't really considered if Nick might be lonely for company too.

Jasper's grin is the only warning we get that he's about to say something he shouldn't. "Don't worry about the chair taking your weight. I've sat right there on Cole's lap plenty of times, rocked back and forth on it too, and it's not given out yet."

Twin patches of color stain the visible part of Nick's cheeks as he looks down at the chair, then back at me with an uncomfortable grimace. "Thank you for that... information. Glad to know the chairs are sturdy."

Natalie puts her hands on her hips. "For fuck's sake, you guys are making this awkward. It doesn't have to be. Look, I don't know the whole complex history between you guys, but here's what I do know. Cole has never taken a day off and Nick was concerned, so he brought soup. Am I right?"

Nick and I look at each other and nod.

"And from what I've gathered, you guys don't really know each other that well on a personal level, so this is weird. But weird we can work with. So we're going to hang out over breakfast and talk. As you like to say Cole, 'use your words.' Now, thank Nick for the kind gesture and ask him how he likes his pancakes."

Silence follows for a couple of seconds before I mumble my genuine gratitude. "Thanks, Nick."

Jasper's shoulders bounce so roughly with his silent laughter that a snort escapes from me. Nick's deep chuckles join mine and soon the whole kitchen is filled with laughter.

We fall into easy conversation as we personalize our pancakes. We work our way through the spread of toppings ranging from jams, chocolate sauce, toffee sauce, maple syrup, bacon, blueberries, strawberries, bananas, marshmallows, and whipped cream. All of us seem to have a sweet tooth, and we recommend different combinations, trying them all until we're stuffed and Nick is patting his stomach.

Nick doesn't have the typical Santa belly that's to be expected from children's books, but he's a bear of a male who likes to stay active, swinging axes and crafting toys with his rough hands rather than being stuck with administrative tasks.

"Can I make anyone some coffee?" Natalie asks as she gathers our empty plates. I smile at how natural it feels for her to offer, how at home she is in my house, and I sit back to take in the view.

"I'll take a caffè mocha again, please," I answer, shoulders feeling somewhat less stiff than before.

"Me, too." Jasper takes the dishes from Natalie and stacks them by the sink.

Heading over to the coffee maker, Natalie asks, "Where do you keep that gingerbread whipped cream? I want some of that again."

"We ran out," I say flatly, not offering any explanation in front of Nick. Natalie will understand soon enough.

Her brows climb up her forehead, but something on my face must give away that I don't want to talk about it right now. "Okay. No whipped cream," she says neutrally, then turns to Nick. "How about you, Santa?"

Ears turning a bright red, Nick says, "A glass of milk, please."

"Seriously?" Natalie asks, genuinely curious and with the cutest grin adorning her face.

Nick's shoulders curl forward and he winces. "Unfortunately, some of those Santa rumors are true. No escaping the milk-appreciating genes."

Natalie's understanding nod is kind and she doesn't poke any further. Instead, she redirects the conversation. "Cole, you and Nick go get comfortable in the living room while Jasper and I make the drinks. Won't we, Jasper?"

Jasper nods excitedly and I get up, gesturing for Nick to precede me to the living room.

9

Natalie

"I don't think I've gotten a proper morning greeting from you yet," Jasper says, pressing his body against my back. His hands snake around my waist and he pulls me to him. Unable to resist, I press my ass back and rub against his cock, which seems to have the inability to ever go soft.

"I hope this got taken care of last night, otherwise you must be in pain," I say over my shoulder, meeting Jasper's hungry eyes.

He runs his nose up the column of my neck and nips at my ear. A shudder works its way down my spine and I tilt my head back, granting him more access. Jasper presses soft kisses against my skin, then drags his teeth along certain spots, making my pussy wetter with each pass.

I turn in his arms and his hands settle on my hips. My fingers climb up his broad chest until I cup the back of his neck.

"Morning," I whisper, craning my neck back to stare at the lips I dreamed about all night.

"I really want to kiss you," Jasper says hoarsely, fingers tightening with his admission.

"Then why don't you?"

"I don't want to scare you." The pained words are soft, between a whisper and a breath.

Something uncomfortable pinches in my chest, and my heart starts pattering away.

No, these aren't feelings. They're just... misplaced pussy flutters.

"Jasper, I already told you I think you're hot. But you're also kind, considerate, funny, and *very* attentive. How can I be scared of you? Is there something else—besides your monster cock, which I'm salivating for—that I should know about?"

The nod Jasper gives me is tiny and unsure.

"Tell me. Or better yet, show me," I encourage.

A muscle ticks in his jaw, but slowly he relaxes and opens his mouth, sticking out his tongue. It keeps coming and coming, past his chin, until the middle of his chest. I swear I feel an actual drop of arousal drip from my pussy at the sight.

"Jasper," I rasp, "that is incredible. I want that in my mouth, but more than anything, I want to feel it shoved up my soaking pussy. I want you to taste how wet you're making me, lick it all up, and swallow it down."

Without another word, Jasper hitches me onto the counter behind me, spreads my legs so they're bracketing his hips, and cups my face. "I'm going to kiss you now. Save those thoughts for when Nick is gone, because I have plans for this pussy." He cups me over my leggings, his touch possessive. "*Our* pussy."

Before I can form a reply that it's actually *my* pussy, Jasper slants his mouth over mine, parting my lips with a gentle lick. His tongue is strong, pointed, and rougher than a human's.

I want more.

I open eagerly for him and kiss him with all my pent-up lust since that first moment I saw him. Our tongues meet and twine, pushing and pulling, going on and on until we're both panting for breath.

I drag him closer, skating my fingers around his neck, up the sides of his face. Breaking our kiss, I whisper against his lips, "Can I touch your horns?"

"Yes." Jasper angles his head, kissing along my jaw, as I trail my fingers along one horn.

"Are they sensitive?"

"The bases are where they meet my temples, but the rest aren't."

"Here?" I ask, tracing a ring around the base above his left eye. A shudder rolls through Jasper and he thrusts his hard cock against my damp leggings.

Resting his forehead against mine, Jasper says, "We have to stop now or I'm going to fuck you right here while Nick is in the next room. I don't think either of us want that. So let's make the drinks and save Cole from the awkwardness of whatever is happening in the living room. Then, once Nick is gone, I'm going to stick this tongue in your wet cunt until you make a mess of my face. Okay?"

"Okay," is all I'm able to manage with that picture in mind.

Jasper helps me down and we silently set to work, taking care not to brush against each other so we don't end up fucking on the kitchen counters.

When we finally make it to the living room, there's a feeling of camaraderie between Nick and Cole, but I sense they're just making small talk, not getting into bigger issues that are keeping them apart.

I'm no expert on familial relationships, but it seems that both of them could do with some companionship. What if they both want to hang out with the other, but have never felt bold enough to suggest it?

Since I've got no skin in this game and will be leaving soon anyway, who better to call them out on their shit than me?

"So, Nick. What's life like being Santa?"

Nick clears his throat and rubs a hand down his beard. "It's good. What's not to like about it? I get to make Christmas wishes come true." His answer sounds sincere and there's warmth in his eyes, but I also sense a hint of sadness. I wonder if he has any Christmas wishes and if there's anyone helping *him* make them come true.

Not about to get derailed by compassion, I turn the conversation to the males I'm a little invested in. "How do you feel about the Naughty List?"

From somewhere next to me, Jasper sucks in an audible breath. I don't look at anyone but Nick, too nervous to find disappointment, hurt, or anger on their faces.

Nick's anxious tick becomes more apparent as that hand of his works overtime on his beard. "It's well... I don't think I've given it much thought. It's just the way things have always been done. It serves a purpose, balances the good and bad."

Deciding to ignore the death glare I'm getting from Cole, I push some more. "Don't you think it's an outdated system? I mean, do you take into account that kids from rougher backgrounds act out more because they're not receiving the right support? Getting shitty coal in their stockings will definitely not motivate them to be better people." I feel like my argument makes great sense and he'd be a fool not to consider it.

Nick's hand pauses on his beard, eyes growing wide as the realization of my words begin to sink in. He looks at

Cole whose face remains impassive, not giving any of his own emotions away.

"Jingle my balls," Nick sighs out spiritlessly. "I didn't think about it in that way. Cole, what are your thoughts?"

Cole gives me a look that says we'll have words later, but I do not regret bringing this up. I know I'm new here, but I'm not okay with people being mistreated. Especially kids. If they're not in a position to fight for themselves, I will gladly fight for them. And in some ways, I think no one has fought for Jasper and Cole either.

Crossing his arms over his chest, Cole chickens out with a weak answer. "I think the system could be improved upon."

Apparently, I'm not done interfering. "What is the ratio of kids on the Naughty List staying on the Naughty List after receiving coal? Do any of them make it onto the Nice List? If so, how many?"

Nick looks at me like I've just thrown a snowball in his face, and Cole looks like he's about to throw one at me.

Deciding to rock the boat with one final question that might change everything, I drop the biggest bomb of all. "Did you know that Jasper and Cole hate being in charge of the Naughty List?"

10

Jasper

Oh shit, did Natalie really just drop those questions like a lit match and then excuse herself to her room before the bomb could go off?

The silence following her exit is louder than any argument. An icy fist squeezes around my heart as I watch Cole war with himself, deciding what to say and what *not* to say.

Despite his bad-boy image, he's a softy and doesn't like making any trouble. The relationship between Nick and Cole is also fairly fragile. Over all my time I've spent in the North Pole, never has Nick visited Cole's house.

Maybe Natalie has been sent by the fates as a catalyst to get us out of the rut we've found ourselves in.

"Cole, I need to know," Nick starts, bracing his forearms on his knees. "Is it true? Do you not like working on the Naughty List?"

Cole closes his eyes for a moment before he opens them again, determination brimming from every pore of his body. "Honestly, it's a fucking shit job."

"Tell me how you really feel," Nick says dryly.

Like a popped balloon, the tension fizzes out of the room.

I'm the first to succumb to laughter, Nick following, and Cole finally joining.

When we're calm enough to talk again, Nick asks, "Is there something specific you would rather do? Or do you have an idea of how we can remake the Naughty List so that it makes sense?"

"Jasper?" Cole throws the ball in my court and I can't help but feel flattered that he wants me to take the lead.

Knowing this is a unique opportunity that might not come again easily, I try to be brave like Natalie would want me to be, building on the foundation she created by opening up this conversation.

"I think we could replace the coal with something else. Something inspirational that would motivate children to try harder, to learn about different perspectives, to give them hope."

Nick nods and clicks his beefy fingers in my direction. "That's great thinking, Jasper. The world would be a much better place if we could uplift those that need it, instead of punishing them. If we could find the right 'thing' it might even lead to a much shorter Naughty List."

I didn't realize I was holding my breath, waiting for his response, until it escapes in a whoosh. "That's the hope."

Nick shifts in his seat to face Cole more directly. "What are your thoughts?"

Biting his lip, Cole's brow puckers before relaxing. "I agree with Jasper. I'm not sure what we can replace it with, but it could make a huge difference in the lives of children and even future generations."

Nick suddenly stands, his large form taking up most of the space in the living room, before he becomes self-conscious. With my horns, I'm usually the tallest in a room, but Nick makes even me feel small.

Nick sits back down, but balances on the edge of the

cushion, excitement twinkling in his eyes. "I've got an idea. How about you guys go on a business trip? Take one of the sleighs, travel around the North Pole, visit the different villages to see what each excels at making, get inspiration, and get back to me with a proposal. If it seems feasible, then we can start production in time for *this* Christmas."

My jaw almost hits the floor, but I'm not alone in my surprise.

"You'd really be okay with that?" Cole asks.

Brows drawing together, Nick looks at us as if the answer should be obvious. "Of course. I don't want you to be unhappy, and seeing children unhappy literally makes me sad. I'm all about good feelings."

I raise a hand. "Can we take Natalie?"

Nick taps a finger against his lips. "How long is she staying with you? I still don't know how a human got in here, nor do I know what's going on between you three, but I think she's good for you—both of you. Don't let her slip through your fingers."

I toy with a horn, then realize I'm giving away my nerves, and fold my hands on my lap instead. "I'm not sure how much we can say, especially because we don't have all the answers yet either. But basically, I met her a couple of days ago and we have this magical bond that forces us to stay close to each other. We don't know how long it'll last, so I hope it's okay that she comes with us."

"Is she bonded to both of you?" Nick asks without a hint of emotion.

"No," Cole says, a careful mask in place that I'm guessing runs in the family, now that I'm seeing them together.

"Not yet," I correct.

Nick's smile is wistful as he says, "How incredibly fortunate you two are. Maybe I'll get lucky and have someone inexplicably bonded to me, too. I can only hope they fight as fiercely for me as Natalie is fighting for you. She has the potential to change your lives."

I swallow hard and realize how true that is. Nick never dates. Just works and makes toys, and keeps everyone around him happy. I hope he'll have someone sent along his way soon, because I'm not sharing Natalie. I also suspect Nick might perhaps be a little scared of her too.

Nick slaps his palms to his knees, his lips pressing into a thin line before he takes a deep breath. "Anyway, I best be going. Got a new line of toys they're doing up at Pyörä I want to oversee. I'll send over one of my sleighs tomorrow morning so you can get going sooner rather than later. Would you mind sending me a plan of your route? I'd love to follow along on your adventure. Maybe check in a time or two?"

"Yeah, no problem. We can definitely do that," Cole says. I sense lots of bonding coming between these two brothers. Natalie might have put more in motion than she set out to do.

All of us stand and I move to Cole's side when Nick asks, "Would a month be enough time for this trip? I think that's the maximum amount of time I can give you before we would need to start production on whatever you pick, if we're planning to get things done by Christmas."

I place an arm around Cole's shoulders. Thankfully, he's not nervous or stiff, just leans into me as the shock of the visit most probably has thrown his defenses off.

"Yes. Definitely. That's really generous. Thank you," Cole says, gratefulness for his big brother shining in his eyes.

"Maybe spending time in the villages will also give the other elves the opportunity to get to know you. To see what a great male you are."

Cole shakes his head. "Yeah, let's not get ahead of ourselves. One thing at a time."

We see Nick out and promise to keep in touch.

11

Cole

The door snicks shut behind me and I take a moment to lean against it, dragging in a fortifying breath as I sift through everything that has happened this morning.

There's a lightness in me that I didn't know stemmed from how much I dread my work, and Natalie has gone and shifted the trajectory of my—*our*—lives, all in the span of a single conversation.

Today was monumental, both in terms of my relationship with Nick, as well as my career. I don't think Natalie has any idea how seriously Nick takes others' happiness and that he will do everything in his power to help me and Jasper. By speaking up, she helped me shave years off my plan to breach the topic.

Still, I can't decide if I'm annoyed that she said something without consulting either of us, or grateful for charging ahead and possibly realigning our lives.

"Where's Natalie?" I ask Jasper when I finally feel like I have a grip on my emotions, needing to share with her that we're leaving in the morning.

"I think she's in her room. She most likely wanted to give us space to talk to Nick."

My bare feet thud against the floors as I make my way toward Natalie's bedroom, Jasper hot on my heels. He slips in front of me as I enter the hallway leading to her room. Placing a hand on the center of my chest, lines of worry form on his face.

"Cole, don't be angry at her. I think she really tried to help. Maybe it was a tad more abrupt than you had planned, but surely this is a good thing? We're going on an adventure!" Jasper tries to reason.

Something melts in my cold heart at Jasper's concern for Natalie. My shoulders slump and I rest my forehead against his shoulder. "I know. I'm not angry, perhaps I was annoyed there for a second that she risked my relationship with Nick, but I'm grateful to her for saying something we've been dancing around and avoiding for years. She just swept in here and changed the course of our lives in a day."

"Surely that's not a bad thing? What if she's meant to be part of our lives, too?" Jasper asks gently.

I lean back and look at Jasper's face. He's so beautiful. Sweet, considerate, patient, and has the heart of a lion at the center of his being.

"I'm starting to think she is," I say softly, cupping his face and rubbing my thumb along his lips.

Joy sparks in his eyes and a mischievous smile forms on his lips. "You can still make her apologize for overstepping. I'd love to see her pretty lips wrapped around your cock as she chokes out her apology. Save the good news for after."

My own grin kicks up the corners of my mouth. "Better get ready for a show then."

I rap my knuckles against Natalie's door and push it open after hearing her call, "Come in."

Natalie lies on her bed, drawing something in a leather-bound sketchbook. Tucking her pen into an inside pocket, she closes the book before I can make out the image. She ties the string with a calm meticulousness that makes me think she is stalling for time, unsure of what our reactions are to this morning.

What kind of images does she sketch, and what will it take for her to share them with us?

"You boys have a good chat?" Natalie asks as she sits up, putting the sketchbook on the side table and crossing her legs like she has no care in the world.

Jasper slips into the room behind me and slouches comfortably in the chair opposite the bed, shooting me a wink before assuming a nonchalant expression that fools no one.

I can see Natalie's defenses are up, probably expecting me to come in here with guns blazing. Instead, all she'll get is a hard cock ready to be stuffed down her throat. I don't say anything, though, letting her squirm in discomfort until she can't take it anymore.

Crossing her arms over her chest, Natalie raises her chin and says, "If you're waiting for an apology, you're going to wait for a long time. But if you'd like to thank me, I can think of ways that will suffice."

"Tsk-tsk, Natalie. It's cute that you think you're calling the shots here. Jasper and I have some plans for you, and we're going to ask you to be a good girl and follow instructions. Think you can do that for us?"

Natalie is a strong, outspoken woman and I find that extremely attractive. But in the bedroom, I need to be in charge. I want to—no, *need* to—see if Natalie will be able to follow directions, if she feels safe enough with me to give up control.

Her eyes narrow at me for a second before she closes them, breathes in deeply through her nose, and visibly relaxes on the exhale. She opens her eyes and playfulness replaces her earlier guardedness, and there's also a hint of challenge in the quirk of her mouth.

"Good girl," I whisper under my breath. This is exactly where I want her.

I take a step forward and brush the hair out of her face. "Natalie, Jasper has a suggestion for how you can apologize for overstepping earlier." With my hand remaining on her face, I incline my head to Jasper. "Tell her."

I glance at him as he scoots forward in his seat, bouncing a little in anticipation for what's to come. His voice is near giddy, almost tripping over the words when he says, "I think you'd look especially beautiful apologizing with Cole's cock down your throat, with drool dripping from those pretty lips as he fucks your face, and your eyes rolling back in your head when you get to taste him for the first time. He tastes sooo good, Natalie. I can't wait for you to find out."

Natalie's lips part and her breathing turns shallow. Her pupils expand until only the tiniest sliver of icy blue remains as her eyes jump between Jasper and me.

Seeing her desire so clearly, I feel I can push a little more. "Jasper paints such a pretty picture, but if you're not sure…"

"Take your monster cock out and show me what I'm working with." Natalie tries to order me, staring unabashedly at the outline of my hard cock.

I shake my head at her boldness, feeling my balls draw up as I anticipate the push and pull between us until she finally surrenders to me.

Slipping my thumb into her mouth, Natalie closes her cherry-red lips around it and automatically sucks, inadvertently quieting herself.

"Get on your knees." Before the rumbling words are even fully out of my mouth, Natalie slips off the bed and her knees sink into the plush cream carpet. Challenge remains in the set of her shoulders as she crosses her arms across her chest and assumes a bored expression. She's such a dichotomy, one moment challenging me, yet also submitting so beautifully. The perfect brat.

Jasper rubs his cock over his pants and his other hand strays toward his belt. I hold up a single finger to stop his progress. "You can watch and you can touch yourself, but that's all. Don't you dare come. Today, Natalie is going to learn what krampus cum tastes like. If she doesn't guess the flavor, you'll just have to come in her mouth again and again until she gets it right."

"That doesn't really sound like a hardship to me," Natalie says with a delectable little smirk on her face that's inviting trouble.

I shake my head and chuckle. "You have no idea how much cum Jasper's got in one load. But you'll learn soon enough. Right now, I want to hear your apology muffled around a mouthful of my cock."

I'm about to ask if she consents, but the bratty woman beats me to it. "Do your worst," Natalie dares me, then opens her mouth wide and sticks her tongue out for me, eager for my cock.

"Little vixen," I say affectionately before shifting to serious again. "Tap my leg if you need a breath, but otherwise, you're going to take this cock and suck it like it's the best thing you've ever tasted. Got it?"

She gives me one nod before I unzip my pants.

"Oh! Me likey!" Natalie says, losing her cool nonchalance the second she sees my cock. "Is that a candy cane wrapped around a Christmas tree, or are you just happy to see me?"

I fist my hard cock, running a hand around the thick veins spiraling from the base to the tip—one of the physical manifestations of my Christmas-elf genetics. I'm already leaking precum at the sight of her so eager for a taste.

Choosing not to respond to her very accurate description of my cock, I grip my wide base, and push into her warm mouth. I don't wait for her to get comfortable, but keep pushing until I meet the back of her throat.

"Look at these pretty lips stretched around my monster cock. Doesn't she look beautiful, Jasper? Think she can take more?"

Jasper's reply is a raspy "yes" and I quickly glance over at him. His gaze is riveted on where my cock is entering Natalie's mouth, his chest heaving as he absentmindedly runs a hand up and down his gloriously thick shaft, pearly liquid already dripping down from his slit.

"Open nice and wide for me, Natalie. Relax that throat and swallow me down." This time, I keep pushing until her lips are wrapped around the girthy base of my cock. I remain there as the cool blues of Natalie's eyes hold me captive, more so than her mouth. My heart beats erratically and a sensation builds in the base of my spine, warning me that this might be over too soon if she keeps looking at me the way she is.

When I go to pull back, wanting to give her a chance to catch her breath, Natalie reaches around me, gripping my bare ass and holding me in place. Her watery eyes stay on me as she swirls her tongue around the underside of my cock, sucking, giving me all she's got.

Realizing I need to wrestle back control before I fall for this woman just as hard as I've fallen for Jasper, I ease up. This time, Natalie allows it. I wrap her hair in my fist before thrusting in again slowly, repeating the motion steadily as her slurping and gagging noises fill the room, right along with little pants from Jasper's corner.

"So pretty when you're choking on my cock. Are you ready to apologize now?"

A jumble of sounds come from her throat and I throw my head back, groaning as the vibrations run against my cock.

"One more time, Natalie. That felt so good." From behind me comes a whimper, Jasper living in the moment just as much as we are.

Natalie's eyebrows twitch—in delight or challenge, I can't quite tell. She cups my balls in one hand, and bobs up and down on my cock. She repeats her apology, but maximizes the effect by elongating the vowels, drawing grunts from me as the nails on her other hand sink into the flesh of my ass.

This woman is a dream. Not just with the way she's sucking me like I really am the best thing she's ever tasted, but she brings a fresh perspective to our lives. She's bold and brave and beautiful, and she challenges me—*us*—in a whole new way.

I withdraw from Natalie's mouth with a pop, needing a moment to compose myself before this is over too soon.

"Jasper, come here. I think Natalie wants a taste," I say a bit more breathlessly than I intended to sound.

Jasper nearly stumbles over his own feet in his haste to get to my side. His hard cock is in one hand, his other hand holding his pants up around his knees.

Natalie grins at him when he stops in front of her, but her eyes quickly widen as they settle on the girth of his shaft and the steady stream of precum dripping from the swollen head.

"Holy fuck. You're a big boy, aren't you, Jasper? Can I lick that thick cock, pretty please?" Natalie rasps, sounding slightly more desperate to taste him than she probably intended.

Jasper nods but doesn't move closer. "Just, um, please don't try to fit it all in your mouth. I know it's big and I don't want you to hurt yourself. It's okay if you just lick around the tip."

My heart aches at the sweetness between them. I've never

been able to fit my own mouth around Jasper's cock, but I've worked it well enough to know how to get him off with licks and nibbles and my hands. The fact that he paused so close to Natalie's mouth to think of her comfort first, is exactly one of the reasons I love him—even if I've never said those words out loud before.

Natalie's smile turns soft before she shores herself up again. "Don't go dropping challenges like that. Let me try."

"I'm not going to let you hurt yourself," Jasper says and almost takes a step back.

Deciding it's time to take control again, I go to stand behind Jasper and wrap my hand around the base of his cock, where his knot will swell later. "Natalie's a big girl, she can decide for herself how much she can take. Right, little vixen?"

Without any further words, Natalie inches forward and swirls her tongue around the head of Jasper's cock. Her eyes pop open and she sits back again, staring at Jasper with surprise and delight glowing in her face. "Wow! Is it...? Give me more." She goes in for another lick and keeps licking until Jasper is trembling with pleasure.

I smile to myself, because that was my first reaction too. Natalie wraps her hand around mine, and together we work Jasper over. I lodge my cock against the cleft of his cheeks, slowly rubbing up and down, but never pushing in.

Jasper has one hand in Natalie's hair and the other reaching behind him, drawing me closer while he tries not to thrust into Natalie's face. His head is leaned back until he's a panting, whimpering mess between us.

I can't take my eyes off of Natalie as she licks and sucks and swirls and pumps and does everything she can until Jasper's body is strung so tightly, I know it's only seconds before he'll explode.

"Come for us, Jasper," I say and, for some unknown

reason, lift onto my toes to gently bite down on the junction where his neck meets his shoulder.

Following my lead, Natalie lifts her mouth off his cock, a string of drool stretching between them. "Be a good boy and fill my mouth," she purrs.

Jasper gasps, giving two shallow thrusts, and then he's shooting streams of warm cum into Natalie's waiting mouth. She does her best to swallow everything down, but it quickly becomes too much and starts spilling over, running down the sides of her mouth, down her neck, onto her shirt.

I step out from behind Jasper and kneel down next to Natalie. Leaning forward, I lick the last drop of cum from his slit and then bend to lick a stripe up Natalie's neck. With a voraciousness I didn't know I possessed, I kiss her. Jasper's flavor snowballs between us, linking the three of us just as Natalie's flavor had last night.

Natalie breaks the kiss and opens her mouth, showing that she didn't swallow any of Jasper's cum I put in her mouth. She gestures for me to stand up, and then points to my cock and her mouth.

"Oh." All my surprise is conveyed in that single word. I'm intrigued by her creativity and how much she's bringing to this dynamic between the three of us.

Jasper pulls me to stand and he wraps his arms around me from behind, guiding my cock into Natalie's very wet mouth.

"She's a dream," he whispers into my ear. "Topping from her knees, isn't she?"

I can't decide how I feel about that. I've never been topped before, but somehow the idea suddenly sounds appealing.

Knowing I'm not going to last long, I say, "I'm going to fuck your face now, Natalie. Tap my leg once if you agree."

Tap.

"Tap my leg twice if you want me to stop."

Natalie just narrows her eyes at me like I said something ridiculous. When her gaze shifts to determination, I start thrusting.

The sloppy sounds of her sucking me, the image of her lips stretched around my cock and Jasper's cum dripping from the corners of her mouth—it's all too much, too beautiful. I place both hands on the back of her head and thrust three times more, and then I'm coming, shooting ropes of sugar plum cum down her throat before sagging back against Jasper.

"That was fun. Let's do it again," he says, already hard against me.

12

Natalie

I've never been so filthy. Never been covered in so much cum. Never been so wet. Never been as excited as I am at this very moment with these two males standing in front of me with their monster cocks already hard again.

Cole was exquisite, pushing me just the right amount, and taking his pleasure from my mouth like it was created with the sole purpose of serving him. And then Jasper entered the chat with his beast of a cock and blew my mind with how gentle he was and how delicious he tasted. Each of them is unique in their own way, calling to a different part of me that is desperate for more.

I'm in big trouble with these two males, because I just might become addicted to them.

I stare down at the black shirt stretched over my tits, ribbons of cum decorating the material, and I can't help but smile.

Jasper is first to break out of his trance of just staring at me. He falls to his knees and kisses me furiously, hands wrapping around my back. Pulling me to him, he stands up with me in his arms, a feat I'm seriously impressed by. I wrap my legs around his waist as he sits us down on the bed.

"Cole," Jasper breathes as he tears his mouth away from mine, licking up and down my neck with that long tongue of his. "I need to make her come more than I need my next breath. Knowing that we just came, and she hasn't yet, is killing me. Want to help me?"

"I think Natalie deserves that. She did so well with sucking us dry," Cole states matter-of-factly, but I catch the warmth in his gaze. "How do you feel about taking a seat on a throne, Natalie? Want to ride Jasper's face?"

"I thought you'd never ask," is all I get out before I'm pushing Jasper onto his back and crawling up his body.

Cole chuckles and comes around the bed. "Do you maybe want to take these leggings off first?" I'm not sure who he's asking, I'm only focusing on positioning my legs around Jasper's neck in a way that I won't suffocate him, but still getting the most out of the position.

With desperation clinging to every syllable, Jasper says, "I'll get her new ones. Right now, I need my tongue in her cunt too much to wait." He taps my ass and I lift up. Monster-strength fingers tear my leggings right down the center and he rips my thong off.

Before I can process how he managed that feat, Jasper pulls me forward so I'm straddling his face, his arms hooking around my thighs to hold me in place.

Without any preamble, he shoves that long tongue of his into my wet cunt, swirling it, pressing it against my front wall, massaging the spot that has me moaning his name.

"Jasper, right there. So good," I mumble, eyes closed and head thrown back as I rock gently over his face.

Cole cups my face and asks, "Can I take your top off, too? I want to lavish these magnificent tits with attention."

Wordlessly, I lift my arms for him to remove my shirt,

head lolling as Jasper fucks me with his very skilled tongue. Cole takes my shirt and bra off with a tenderness that makes those pussy flutters return to my heart. We hold eye contact for a moment, and I glimpse something in his gaze that's raw yet delicate—something I'll reexamine when I'm not hazy with lust.

A whimper tears from my throat when Cole cups my breasts and pinches my nipples with just the right amount of pressure, while Jasper eats me out like I'm his favorite dessert. I cry out a mixture of both their names as an orgasm slams into me, racking my body with shudders.

While I ride out the aftershocks, Cole holds me steady and Jasper massages my thighs.

Jasper places a gentle kiss against my swollen cunt and groans, "You taste so good. I need more. But first, I want to see to your tits too."

Before I can figure out what's happening, Jasper's grip around my thighs tightens and he rolls over so I'm on my back and he's positioned on top. "Oh, yes! Those are pretty tits. I want to play with them. I want to learn all your sounds. Like..." Jasper gets a devious look in his eyes before he surges forward with one hand and pinches my nipple—hard.

I let out a yelp that quickly transforms into a moan as the pain morphs into pleasure. Jasper repeats the process on the other side and Cole leans down to suck a nipple into his mouth. The two play with my tits until I'm squirming and panting, cresting the hill toward release.

Just before Jasper can shove me over the edge, he stops and sits back on his haunches, a knowing glint in his eye that he's got me right where he wants me. At this point I'm wetter than I've ever been in my life—something that should alarm me, but I can't give a fuck right now.

Spreading my thighs as far as they will allow him, Jasper calls Cole to join him, "Cole, come look at this magnificently wet cunt. Just for us. So slick. Take a lick, I know you want to."

"Since when are you calling the shots?" Cole says without heat and slaps Jasper's ass, adding a squeeze that has Jasper grunting.

"Since this is the best thing I've tasted since I got my first taste of you," Jasper states sweetly, following it with a wink. A whimper tries to escape me at how fucking hot their chemistry is, but I swallow it down not to ruin their moment.

Cole's face softens and there's so much love between them that my heart squeezes uncomfortably. As they stare at each other, I snake a hand down and start rubbing my clit. Jasper's head flicks to the motions and he bats my hand away.

Pointing a finger at me, Jasper scolds, "That's *our* pussy. You don't get to touch until we say you can."

Oooh, who's the bossy one now? A trickle of arousal drips from my cunt and I clench my core muscles, willing it to go back before I make a mess of the bed.

"Jasper, did you see that? Look how much our words are turning her on. I can see her cunt weeping for us. Isn't it, Natalie? Do you need us to touch you more? Is this cunt ours?"

I choose to ignore the questions about possession, and redirect the conversation to more pressing matters. "For fuck's sake, stop teasing. If no one is going to do something about this then I'm going to grab my biggest dildo and do it myself."

"But is your biggest dildo bigger than Jasper?"

I narrow my eyes because it sure as shit isn't. But they don't have to know that.

"Why are we talking so much? Let's get naked," Jasper says and strips his shirt off with an easy practice that doesn't let it catch on his horns. Cole grins and takes his off too.

Jasper pauses and looks at Cole with absolute raw need. "Cole, I need you, too."

Cole's grin is knowing, his eyes holding a fire that gives away how much he loves hearing those words. "How about I fuck this perfect ass while you see how many orgasms you can wring from Natalie?"

Jasper is near giddy as he makes quick work of the rest of his clothes. "Challenge accepted."

Cole follows suit and I, too, strip out of my torn leggings, throwing them in the pile next to the bed.

With everyone naked now, we all take a moment to look our fill, chests heaving with anticipation.

They're absolutely perfect. Cole, covered from neck to wrists to ankles in tattoos that I can't wait to study. Jasper, with only a single tattoo on his thigh that he shares with me, and a sprinkling of chest hair that leads to a happy trail to the biggest cock I've seen in my life.

It's even bigger with the protruding base of his knot that I heard them talking about earlier. I got a quick look at it when he was coming all over my face, but I don't think it had swollen as big as it can get.

I knew I'd been training with dildos for a reason. My mouth might not be able to fit him, but my pussy sure as fuck will.

Cole's cock is beautiful. The veins remind me of a candy cane the way they spiral around the Christmas-tree shaft. Never could I have imagined a shape so unique.

"Lie down, Natalie, and start counting. I want you limp and sated when I'm done with you," Jasper says as he maneuvers me onto my back.

I prop myself onto my elbows and lift a single brow. "I love the enthusiasm, but no one has managed to make me come more than twice in one night. That's a skill only I've done to myself."

The absolute feral looks in the males' eyes has me rethinking my taunt. On the other hand, I deserve to be worshiped.

Cole walks over to the nightstand and takes out a bottle of lube. The sound of the lid popping open has my pussy clamping down on nothing. I'm damn near panting as Cole coats his cock generously while his gaze roams over our bodies.

Jasper doesn't wait a second longer and dives forward with renewed vigor, swirling his very skilled tongue around my clit and crooking his fingers in my cunt. I hold onto his horns as my second orgasm of the day barrels into me with the force of a high-speed train before Cole has even started fucking Jasper.

Every so often, Jasper groans with pleasure, causing him to lose focus when Cole preps him with his fingers. He lifts his mouth off my cunt and breathes deeply, hands squeezing on my thighs as Cole finally slides in, both of them sighing in pleasure when Cole bottoms out.

For some reason, both of them settle their satisfied gazes on me at that moment. Being made part of such an intimate experience almost makes me curious about what it would feel like to trust someone so completely, to allow someone to love me the way they love each other.

Soon, I'm forgetting all my sappy thoughts as I'm screaming their names. Cole pounds into Jasper with long, hard strokes that shift the whole bed, driving Jasper's tongue deeper into my cunt.

"That's it, Jasper, eat that sugar cookie cunt. Listen to how sweetly you're making Natalie scream," Cole grunts between thrusts. "She's so beautiful with your krampus tongue fucking her cunt."

Spurred on by Cole's praise, Jasper slides a slick finger into my ass. I come again, fireworks setting off behind my closed eyelids and fizzing through my veins. Jasper never lets up though, guiding me through my orgasm as Cole gentles his thrusts for a minute.

When I'm adequately returned to my faculties, Cole picks up the pace again and drives into Jasper with forceful thrusts that have the male whimpering in pleasure.

"Good boy, look how well you take my cock. This ass was made for me," Cole praises Jasper. The sweetness of his words combined with the power of the sounds he's drawing out of Jasper, plus the sensations coursing through my body, has me nearly out of my mind.

Somewhere around orgasm six, I lose count, no longer able to hold myself up to watch them come together so exquisitely.

With a shout, Jasper lifts his face from my cunt and pulls me down so my legs wrap around both of them. He pumps his hand up and down his cock in time with Cole's thrusts, covering me in streaks of white cum, decorating me like the happiest gingerbread cookie there ever was.

Cole follows soon after, emptying himself into Jasper on a hoarse cry. Together, the three of us collapse in a tangle of limbs onto the bed in a sticky, blissed-out, sated mess.

"I can get used to this." I didn't mean to say those words aloud, but the way the males mumble their agreement makes a tiny little snowflake perch on my heart, some unnamed emotion I've never felt slowly warming my veins.

13

Jasper

After that explosive session in Natalie's room, we take turns in the shower to get clean, not trusting ourselves to be naked together for a while yet. There's this excessive need to be constantly touching, to be as close as we can get to each other, *in* each other.

I'm craving to feel Natalie's wet heat wrapped around my cock, but I'm not rushing that process. I know I'm much bigger than average, however, trying to take me might be a challenge that our adventurous Natalie would enjoy.

Cole and I have never tried it either, him preferring to top me and I'm very okay with that, but I can't help the deep-seated need I have to one day also let him give up a little control and let me fuck him—with lots of prep, of course.

"Night," Natalie calls, peeking into the bedroom I share with Cole and waving at me like she's about to go sleep on her own.

I frown. "Where do you think you're going?"

"My room," she answers like it's obvious and I'm the one being obtuse here.

"I don't think your bed is in any state to be slept in tonight. That thing is soaked and filthy," I point out.

Natalie's voice is falsely cheerful when she counters, "If you show me where the sheets are, then I can quickly change them."

Cole comes up behind Natalie and wraps his arms around her waist, walking her into our bedroom. Thankfully, she doesn't resist and I note the small smile playing on her lips.

She likes all the affection.

I'm going to affection her so hard she can't help but fall in love with both of us.

Cole guides her onto the bed and props a bottle of water in her hands. "Hydrate. Please." He reaches for another bottle and gives me one of my own. "You too. The amount of fluid that came from your bodies will need to be replenished."

Natalie takes a couple of gulps of water, then says, "Honestly, I've never come so many times in one day."

I sit up a bit straighter, my chest puffing out with pride at that statement. "We can always see if we can beat this record." I pull her into my lap and nuzzle her neck. She burrows into me and Cole sits down with us, leaning his head on my shoulder and placing a hand on her thigh.

"I can't believe I'm saying this, but I think you've gotten as much out of me as I can possibly give. It was amazing, but there's no way I can come again tonight."

Cole brushes up and down her leg in a comforting caress and Natalie's body relaxes into me. This right here, is perfect. The three of us feel like magnetic puzzle pieces finally coming together. Logically, I know it doesn't make sense because Natalie is new to our dynamic, but it just works.

Cole traces the tattoo on Natalie's thigh, fingers lingering on the new symbol she shares with me. "You missed a big part of the chat earlier, with Nick. I was going to tell you when he left, but well—" He shrugs and his eyes roam up from her thighs and settle on her breasts for a moment before making eye contact. "—we had other priorities."

Hooking her leg over Cole's, Natalie looks a bit sheepish. "I hope I didn't fuck things up for you or make it too awkward with Nick. That wasn't my intention."

Cole huffs a laugh. "You just might have changed our lives."

Natalie's widened eyes soften when she registers Cole's tone, hope traveling across her face like a shooting star. "Yeah?"

Deciding to join in and put her out of her misery, I say excitedly, "Because of you, we're going on an adventure! Tomorrow!"

"That's great. You and Cole?" Natalie asks hesitantly, her smile unsure.

My brows draw together and I squeeze her tighter to me. "You too, gorgeous." Resting my forehead against hers, I add, "We're kind of stuck together, in case you forgot."

Natalie leans back and looks between Cole and me, her expression guarded but optimistic. "Really? Where are we going?"

With a sparkle in his eyes, Cole explains, "So, maybe Jasper told you some of this already, but Joulu is our central town, and then we have a bunch of villages too. Each village excels at different skills and is responsible for different types of toy production. There's carpentry in Puutyöt, wheeled toys in Pyörä, soft toys in Pehmolelu, books in Kirja, and so on. Our mission is to go around searching for inspiration, and to get back to Nick with an idea or product that can replace coal for those on the Naughty List."

Natalie sits up straighter, the corners of her mouth turning down. "So the Naughty List isn't going anywhere?"

Shaking his head, but remaining hopeful, Cole says, "Not yet. But, if we can come up with an adequate replacement, maybe we can inspire kids and the Naughty List can get shorter and shorter."

Natalie reaches forward and squeezes Cole's hand. "That's amazing. And Nick's on board with all of this?"

There's something so natural about them, a connection that has my pulse thickening and speeding up at the same time. They're *it* for me, now to just make them realize they're *it* for each other too.

Cole's smile is bright and unburdened, a look I long to see on him every day. "It was his idea to see us off as soon as possible. He's sending a sleigh for us in the morning. Tonight, I want to plan the route and we'll keep him updated on our progress."

I graze my lips against Natalie's ear as I whisper, "Are you ready to see how Christmas elves make toys? Want to see what year-round Christmas looks like?"

Natalie looks down, admitting shyly, "I've never had a real Christmas before, so this feels like it's making up for all of that."

"Neither have we," Cole admits. In his eyes, I see him flit through so many memories of us over the years. We have never felt like we can celebrate the day when we feel so guilty for ruining it for others.

Usually, around Christmas, I don't feel up to having company. When the day comes around, I'm still reeling from having been stuck in my shifted form and being nearly feral. At that point, I just sit alone in my cabin in the mountains and write children's stories with happy endings to replace the reality of what they had just faced, even if no one will ever read them.

We take a moment for our joint admissions about our shitty Christmases to sink in, then Cole gets up to grab his laptop. Together, the three of us plan the route and share ideas for which village we should visit first, what possible toys could inspire children to get off the Naughty List, and what we need to pack.

When it gets late into the night, Cole closes his laptop. "I think it's time we get some sleep. We have a lot to do tomorrow."

Natalie makes to get up and I koala hug her to me. "You can't leave. I need you to cuddle me all night. I usually like to be the small spoon, but tonight I want to be the filling in the sandwich." I pout and give her the best puppy dog eyes I can muster, and a smile kicks up at the corner of her mouth.

"You're lucky you're so cute," she says and playfully pokes me in the side.

Stark naked, Cole climbs onto the bed behind me. "I hope you don't mind, but I hate sleeping in clothes," he tells Natalie.

Natalie's eyes go uncharacteristically dopey as her gaze travels up and down Cole's body, studying his tattoos. "I don't mind one bit," she sighs out lustily. Pointing to the swans swimming around his biceps on his right arm, she asks, "What are these?"

"Ah, this is part of my ode to 'The Twelve Days of Christmas.' They're the 'seven swans a-swimming.'"

"It's like a treasure map. You should try to find them all," I encourage.

Natalie's eyes light up and she climbs out of my arms to study the design more closely. She traces each swan, lifts Cole's arm this way and that to see the tiny details of their feathers, before moving on to the next tattoo.

I kneel next to her and, together, we point out different tattoos, tracing over them with gentle fingers while Cole lies back with his fingers locked behind his head, basking in all the attention.

"This one is my favorite," I say and caress the band of

nutcrackers drumming down his left side. Goose bumps dot Cole's body and a lazy grin takes over his face.

"They're beautiful," Natalie says and her hand joins mine, fingers moving in a way that looks like she's trying to memorize every detail of not just the design, but Cole too.

"They are," I echo, but my eyes settle on Cole's. There's a sparkle in his gaze that I'm certain is reflected in my own.

"Oh, 'three French hens,'" Natalie says, fingers gliding over Cole's thigh.

My eyes snag on something peeking out between the hens, and my breath grows hot and tight in my throat. I bite my lip to keep the quiver hidden, but somehow, both of them notice it.

"What is it?" Natalie asks gently, laying a hand on my shoulder.

My eyes get misty as I stare into Cole's dark gaze, feeling a surety that I was lacking until now. "Cole's got our matching tattoo."

14

Cole

Sitting up, I stare at the tattoo hidden between my three French hens. "When did I get this?" I'm not sure how long it's been there. I hardly inspect my thighs on a daily basis.

"Maybe when we arrived? Couldn't have been before that, since the distance limit wouldn't have allowed it," Jasper suggests, thumb idly stroking over the tattoo.

"I didn't feel the moment I got mine either," Natalie explains. "I just noticed it when I was sitting on the couch in the middle of a meeting on the island. When I noticed it, it kind of triggered everyone into searching their bodies for their own markings. Those with markings in the same spot are bonded."

"It makes sense for you two to have it, since you were there at the same time. But why me? Why now?" I'm too nervous to get excited, scared it might be a mistake of some sort, but a tiny part of me is holding on to the hope that I'm just as much a part of this inexplicable connection and bond now.

"Let me call Bertie and ask him. Maybe he knows," Jasper

says in what I'm assuming is a reassuring smile, but his pure joy is hard to hide when his eyes are shining so brightly.

Not waiting a moment longer, Jasper gets up and searches for his phone among his luggage, and dials Adelbert. I almost want to ask him to put the call on speaker, but I know Adelbert would not like that much, so I content myself with waiting patiently for him to finish—my heart beating erratically all the while.

Seemingly aware that I need to be distracted, Natalie straddles my hips and my hands automatically settle on her delicious thighs. I stroke up and down her skin, watching my fingers glide over the band of tattoos circling her thigh, and over our shared tattoo.

My fingers get greedy, and I start kneading her thighs, sinking my fingers into her flesh, and wondering how she likes to be gripped. Her subtle rocking has my cock growing hard, and a smirk spreads across her lips when she feels it against the thin layer of her tiny sleep shorts.

Natalie places a finger against my lips, letting me know I have to be quiet while Jasper is on the phone. I give her a nod, then she braces her hands on my chest and grinds down hard on my cock.

My stomach muscles contract and I grit my teeth against the sensation. I've already come twice and I don't know if I'm able to come again, but Natalie looks set on trying to get me there.

Still on the phone, Jasper comes to stand at the side of the bed and stares down at us with uncontained desire. He rubs his cock through his loose pajama pants, but the look he gives me turns devilish. Pulling his cock free, he holds it in front of my face and mouths, "Lick."

Not knowing when these two teamed up, I open my mouth obediently and lick a delicious drop of gingerbread cum from Jasper's slit. He rolls his lips between his teeth to keep a sound from escaping, but his eyes roll back in his head as I shower his cock with attention.

Natalie rocks faster and faster, my fingers digging into her ass to help her set a rhythm, but there's no controlling her right now. Not her, and not Jasper.

My heartbeat ratchets up, slamming against my chest, drumming through my whole body, until I'm a big pile of need. I'm not above begging at this stage, but I'm trying to keep from making any sounds.

I want to shove Natalie's shorts aside and plunge into her, but not like this. When I take her cunt, I want to hear her scream.

Jasper keeps his answers short, Adelbert seemingly doing the heavy lifting in the conversation, and I double down on his cock. Making eye contact with him, I spit on his cock and wrap my hand around him and squeeze. His breath stutters and mine becomes shallow.

"Yes, thank you. I'll tell them. We'll chat tomorrow on the video call then. Bye," Jasper says into the phone and then he's flinging it across the room with a wild look in his eyes.

"Look how well you're sucking this cock, Cole. But telling by the veins bulging in your neck, you need to come real soon. Doesn't he look sweet like this, Natalie? Naked beneath us while we toy with him?"

"So good," Natalie says with a bright sheen on her cheeks. "Cole is such a good boy for us," she teases.

Not able to stand this any longer, I flip her onto her back. "Good boy, you say? No, no, no, little vixen. You're barking up the wrong tree. I'm going to stuff this cunt with my cock right now and teach you a lesson while you try to suck Jasper's cum straight from his cock. Okay?"

Jasper looks to Natalie with a question in his eyes that he gives voice to. "Are you too sore? We can stop if you need."

"I don't know how or when it happened, but I'm already

good to go. Give me all your cum. I'm tested and on birth control too."

"Us too," I say, and rip her shorts down her legs. Seeing the glistening arousal dripping from her, I know she's ready for me. I drape her legs around me and in one single thrust, plunge my cock into her warm cunt.

Natalie's back bows off the bed and she screams with pleasure, but I'm not done. I thrust hard and fast, and when she's squeezing around my cock like she's about to explode, I stop.

"No! Whyyyy? I was so close," Natalie whines, trying to thrust herself onto my cock.

"Who's a good boy, now?" I taunt. "Up." I pull out of her and position her onto her hands and knees. "Give Jasper your mouth."

Jasper notes my mood and positions himself in front of her, guiding his cock to her mouth, but not pushing in. Natalie's desire to satisfy him pleases me immensely as she lavishes his cock with attention.

On my knees behind her, I pull her cheeks apart. "Tell me, Natalie, how do you feel about anal?"

"Love it," she mumbles, mouth not lifting off Jasper's cock.

"Good. Soon, you'll take me in this tight little hole, while Jasper takes your cunt with his thick cock. You'll be such a good girl taking us both. That's what you really want to be, isn't it?" I tease, knowing it'll rile her up and that she gets off on this talk as much as we do.

Before she can respond, I thrust back into her dripping cunt and fuck her hard. Jasper holds her steady as my thrusts move her too much to keep her mouth on his cock. When her walls squeeze around me again, I pause.

"No. Not again," she sobs and lowers herself onto her elbows. There's no real hurt in her voice, more annoyance.

"I thought you liked edging?" I say and thrust again lightly, caressing her back and appreciating the view from this angle.

"I do," Natalie admits and tightens her muscles around my cock.

"Jasper, come lie down here." I point to the middle of the bed and slowly pull out of Natalie. I see him hesitate and I know he thinks he's too big, that maybe he'll hurt her, but I know without a shadow of a doubt that Natalie can take him.

Every instinct within me, the very essence of my being can admit that somehow the three of us were made for each other. That we fit together in a way that just makes sense. Tattoo or no tattoo, something about us feels right.

I soften my voice, "She can take you, I'm sure of it. Now, hang your head off the side of the bed so I can fuck your throat. Natalie's going to work herself down on your cock at her own pace. Everyone in?"

Natalie sits back on her haunches and looks at Jasper. Pointing to his cock, she says with surety, "That beast will be conquered tonight. I'm so horny and so wet right now, I can take anything. Jasper, you just lie down and I'll do all the work."

Seemingly satisfied with that, Jasper lies back, cock jutting proudly into the air. He really is enormous. And so, so perfect.

Natalie crawls up his thighs and slowly rubs her wet pussy all over him. "I've never been as wet as I've been since I met you two. I don't know what it is, but I'm constantly dripping."

I note the muscles in Jasper's throat bob on a swallow. Why he's suddenly nervous, I'm not sure, but he quickly covers it with, "Maybe that pussy was made to take this cock. The only way to take me was if you were slick with arousal.

And aren't you, Natalie? You're slick for us with your sugar cookie flavor."

"Fuck, yes, I am," Natalie says and notches him at her entrance. Completely entranced, I watch her slowly lower herself down on his cock in incremental movements. Her eyes flutter closed and her chest moves up and down on shallow breaths.

"That's it, Natalie. You're doing so well. Look how beautiful you are stretched around that fat cock. Good girl. Good girl," I croon, leaning forward to stroke her face.

"So. Full. Good. Cock. Perfect," Natalie pants with a dazed smile. Sweat dots her brow as she lifts up an inch before sinking down two more.

"Natalie, you feel so good. This cunt is so tight and warm and wet. You were made for my cock," Jasper grits out. His white-knuckled grip on the blanket is trembling, his pulse erratic in his throat as he watches Natalie's progress.

I lift his hands and place them on Natalie's tits and he starts playing with them, distracting both of them while she makes her way to the hilt.

When her hips are finally flush with his, I place a hand on her lower stomach, the outline of Jasper's cock causing it to bulge. "Look at this. So full. You're gorgeous, the both of you. So good together."

Natalie pants, her eyes wild but happy and a victorious smile stretches her lips until her whole face transforms into satisfaction. "I knew you'd fit," she says and winks at Jasper.

Something odd happens in my chest and travels all the way to my toes. In this moment, I know that I'm already falling for Natalie as deeply as I've fallen for Jasper. A feeling of determination settles deep in my gut as I decide that I will do anything I can to keep them. I will court not only my krampus, but my human too. Make them want to stay and take on life together with me.

Jasper's fingers settle around Natalie's waist, a look of pure awe in his eyes as he says, "You really are made for me. *Us.*"

"She is," I whisper, still amazed at how seamlessly we've come together and how hard I'll fight for our happy ending.

"Cole, take his throat. I'm owning this cock tonight," Natalie directs like the boss she is, lifting off Jasper's cock again before dropping back down. Hard. Jasper gasps and his hands settle around her waist.

I bend forward and give Natalie a sloppy kiss, then move to stand at Jasper's head, stepping carefully between his horns. Tapping his cheek, I say, "Open wide. You know the drill. Tap my leg if you need a breath."

Together, Natalie and I work Jasper over. She rides Jasper's cock like a cowgirl set on winning a rodeo. And Jasper, being the prized bull, gives her as much as he can while I'm holding his throat captive.

Natalie moans, her tits bouncing with her movements. Her cheeks are flushed, her head thrown back in ecstasy but her gaze stays on Jasper's lips around my cock, flicking to my face every now and then.

Together, our bodies create a symphony of carnal sounds as we get lost to speech and give over to sensations.

Noting the clench of Jasper's abs, the cadence of Natalie's breath and the telltale signs of an orgasm building in the base of my spine, I find the words to push us into the abyss of pleasure together.

"Come for me."

I pull out of Jasper's mouth and spray my cum across his chest just as Natalie starts to go limp with her release. Jasper sits up and gathers her into his arms, rolling them so she's on her back. He pulls out a little and wraps his hand around his inflated knot as he pumps her full of cum.

Finally sated, Jasper rolls over and lies on his back, cock slowly going soft as his breathing starts to even out.

I walk around the bed, watching streams of Jasper's delicious cum dripping from Natalie's cunt. As if my brain is unable to control my body, only instinct dictating my moves, I surge forward and start licking Jasper and Natalie's combined releases from between her swollen pussy lips. It's the most exquisite thing I've ever tasted. The perfect mix of sugar and spice.

Natalie's final orgasm of the night is a tiny shudder running through her body and a sigh of contentment escaping from her lips.

I look down at the two beings who couldn't be more different, but somehow hold my heart equally. Something magical occurred tonight, bound us together in some way. I'm not sure what the consequences are yet, but I'm all in with both of them.

Now, just to convince them to pick me too.

15

Natalie

"Holy fuck," I exclaim, my eyes going wide when I catch sight of the red sleigh and the two reindeer out the window. I rush toward the front door, throw it open, and come to a stop with Jasper and Cole flanking me.

My feet are unable to move, my brain unable to compute the sight before me.

Stepping from the sleigh like I'm living out some kind of childhood dream, is Nick—the real-life, actual *Santa*, with a brilliant smile lighting up his whole face. His light eyes twinkle with merriment when he takes in our surprised faces.

Sketching a bow, Nick points to the sleigh with mittened hands. "My lady, dear sirs, your carriage awaits."

I'm still stuck taking in the scene when Jasper shoves his feet into his shoes and bounds toward the sleigh. He runs a hand along the smooth red wood and calls out, "It's our own motherfucking sleigh!"

A joyous rumble starts low in my belly and bubbles through my body, fizzing through my very pores until laughter bursts out of me. I turn to Cole and he's wearing the same excited grin. Impossibly, my joy grows, turning my smile into something goofy as some warm and fuzzy feelings take root deep in my gut. Instead of shunning the feelings as I usually would, I lean into them, letting them spread until I feel like happy endings might just be possible.

Cole must sense something in my expression, his smile morphing into one so sugary sweet I might get a cavity merely looking at it. He bends and helps me with my boots, then laces his fingers with mine. Together, we run toward Jasper, my steps so light and giddy it almost feels like I'm floating across the snow.

Cole and Nick shake hands and Jasper turns, throws his arms around the two of them, and squishes them together. Deciding I want in on the action, I also skip over to them and burrow into the group hug.

I don't know when I became a skipping kind of woman, maybe it's the North Pole having that effect on me. Or it could be all the orgasms from last night and subsequent happy feelings coursing through my veins.

Everyone groans good-naturedly as we hug each other and we dissolve into chuckles. I think this is my first-ever group hug, and weirdly, I kind of like it. There's something so pure about all of us embracing that I can almost picture having more of this in my future.

A reindeer snorts and I'm the first to break away, curious about seeing one up close.

"Can I touch them?" I ask Nick, taking in the pretty harnesses. The bridles around their snouts have lovely intricate stitching in red, green, and gold. The portions leading along their bodies have plaid handmade garlands that almost look like ribbons cut from some of Nick's own clothes. Interspersed between the ribbons are jingle bells. That explains what I heard before I saw them out the window.

"Sure, you'll be spending lots of time with them, so it's good to get you acquainted," Nick says and comes to stand next to me. He runs a hand along the closest reindeer's neck and gives him a loving pat. "This is Merry." Moving to the other reindeer, he introduces her with the same amount of affection, "And this sweetie pie is Jolly."

I scratch along Merry's neck the same way Nick did. "Hi, I'm Natalie. I like your harness. It's giving me ideas," I say and throw a wink at Jasper.

Jasper growls and bites his fist like he's not opposed to the idea. "You know I like the way you ride me. Might give you something to hold on to next time. Cole too." This time, he winks at Cole who arches back an intrigued brow.

Out of the corner of my eye, I glimpse a blush brightening Nick's cheeks, and I swear that's longing in his eyes. I wonder how he'll meet his Mrs. Claus. Hope it's soon, because he really seems like a nice male who would take good care of someone.

Cole inspects the sleigh, walking around it, skimming his hands along the curve of the wood, and across the dark green velvet bench seat. I can almost feel his touch like an invisible hand as I replay how he glided his hands over my body in the same way last night.

Pausing with one hand on the front lip of the sleigh, Cole asks, "Nick, did you build this yourself?"

The color in Nick's cheeks intensifies until he resembles the sleigh. "Uh, yeah. It's a little personal project of mine," he mumbles and rubs the back of his neck. "It's not perfect, and I can't use it for Christmas, obviously it's too small to hold the compartment for my Santa bag with all the presents. But, um, you guys are welcome to use it for however long you need." Nick looks down at his boots and scuffs his heel against the snow in an adorably shy manner. He's like a big teddy bear and I totally get why he's Santa.

Jasper lopes over to him and envelops the bigger man in a hug. "Ah, Nicky. You're the sweetest." Then, he smacks a kiss to Nick's beard-covered cheek before bouncing back over to me by the reindeer, wrapping his arms around my shoulders and pulling me flush against him. I sink into Jasper's touch and lean my head against his chest.

This right here is the most wholesome moment of my life. I have zero worries or frustrations. I'm freshly fucked, standing in the arms of a male who I'm pretty sure I'm developing some not-just-horny feelings for, while the other male who is chipping away at all my carefully constructed walls looks at us with so much warmth that it's making my toes curl in my boots.

Are these fucking heart flutters? I'm so used to pussy flutters that the sensation this far north is catching me off guard. I surprisingly don't mind them as much as I thought I would— or maybe it's only because it's with Jasper and Cole.

Cole shifts his gaze back to Nick and places a hand on his brother's shoulder. "This sleigh is a work of art, Nick. The detailing and the craftsmanship is better than anything I've seen. You must have spent hundreds of hours on this."

"She's a beauty, Nick. Perfect color choice too," Jasper adds, giving my lips a lingering look. I guess Nick and I share a love for the color red.

Nick looks positively bashful with all the compliments and my heart grows about two sizes.

Gaze filled with pure wonderment, Cole says, "It's incredibly kind of you to let us use it, Nick. Thank you. We'll take good care of the sleigh."

"And the reindeer," I add cheerfully, knowing Nick cares even more about them.

Nick rubs at his chest like our words really mean something special to him. "Thank you. Merry and Jolly are a mated pair. Reindeer don't usually take lifelong partners, but these two refuse to be separated. When you get to the villages, please make sure the elves stable them together, otherwise they'd find a way to break through walls to get to each other."

"Noted. They'll be safe and happy with us," Jasper says and playfully salutes Nick.

Thinking of one of the most important factors no one has mentioned, I call out, "Snacks! What kind of snacks do they like?"

Nick lifts a bag from a compartment in the sleigh and hands it to Cole. "These are some special candy canes they enjoy. They're reindeer friendly—the elves figured out a recipe that the reindeer like and won't be too hard on their tummies. You can always stock up in the villages, but I'm guessing the elves will take care of them without you needing to ask for anything. They love all my reindeer."

"Candy canes?" I murmur. "I can think of something else that reminds me of candy canes." At my suggestive tone, Jasper pulls me closer and bends down to bite lightly on my shoulder, nipping his way up my neck.

His breath is hot and wet against my ear as he whispers, "Tonight, when we get to Puutyöt, I want to see Cole's candy-cane cock in your ass. If you can handle that and crave more, I want to stretch your sweet cunt around my fat cock at the same time. I want to feel Cole rubbing against me as we both take you, fill your ass with sugar plum cum and your cunt with—"

"That's my cue to go," Nick says loudly, his ears now the color of the sleigh. Judging from the way he's unable to make eye contact with Jasper and me, I'm guessing he has highly sensitive hearing.

Cole tries to hide his smile, compassion for his highly uncomfortable brother overriding his mirth as he comes to stand with us. As if it's the most natural thing in the world, I slip my right hand into Cole's, and Jasper drapes one arm around Cole's shoulder.

"I'll keep you updated," Cole says. "We're visiting Puutyöt first. Depending on if we find inspiration or not, we'll adjust our stay accordingly. After that, we're heading to Pehmolelu."

"That sounds wonderful," Nick says a little wistfully. Moving to the reindeer to say his goodbyes, Nick pets them and gives them gentle hugs before turning back to us. "You better be off. I've left the skies clear for today's journey, but I'll send some fresh snow for you when you arrive tonight. Might be romantic over there. It's a beautiful village with all their wooden houses and the twinkling lights strung from the eaves, and the..." Nick's eyes glaze over as the picture seemingly forms in his mind. It sounds absolutely magical and I can't wait to go.

Cole goes in for a hug and Nick shocks back into his body. Even though I haven't known them long, there's a stark difference in how they're interacting now versus yesterday. It's the cutest thing to see them building their relationship, and I'm starting to feel like I want to stay here long enough to witness their bond growing.

Jasper steps up to hug Nick and I follow suit. The three of us wave him off as he walks back to town. After this trip, I'm not sure where I'm going to be, but I'm set on reaching out to any single monster fuckers, or monster-curious people, because I want to make it my mission to find someone for Nick.

When Nick's finally out of view, Cole pivots and wraps a hand around Jasper's throat, pulling the taller male down for a filthy open-mouthed kiss that's all tongue and teeth. And just like that, my pussy is soaked. I'm going to have to start carrying a mop around with me when I'm around these two.

Cole reaches out with his free hand and pulls me closer, ripping his mouth from Jasper's and kissing me with the same voraciousness. The kiss steals my breath and my knees literally go weak, so Cole braces me to keep me upright.

Jasper threads a hand into my hair and when I go to pull back from Cole, I feel we're both held in place by Jasper. Bending down, Jasper places his mouth next to ours and joins the kiss with his long krampus tongue. Our three tongues dance and tussle, Jasper's much longer one dominating ours as he takes charge of the sloppy kiss.

When we're sufficiently breathless, Jasper steps back with an obnoxiously satisfied grin pulling up the corners of his mouth. "There's more where that came from."

Jasper practically frolics into the house to grab our bags as I stand there, still too stunned to move. Cole laughs and then he's following Jasper into the house, holding the door open for me with a patient smile.

What is my life even? How did I get here? All I know is that I can't imagine returning to a life without Cole and Jasper.

Natalie: Hey! How's life with your wolf?

Diana: It's… interesting. How's life in the
North Pole?

Natalie: I'm going to need more info on that.
Soon. But things here are pretty spectacular
star-struck emoji

Diana: Yay! That's great! I'm also maybe
going to need advice. Soon.

Natalie: Ooo! Sounds interesting.

Diana: Could be *smirking face emoji* How's
Jasper and the other male you're visiting?

Natalie: They're both pretty great. We're
leaving on a trip together today. Not sure
how long we'll be gone, and I don't know
how good reception is there.

Diana: That sounds like fun! Reception isn't
too stable here either. Please check in
whenever you can.

Natalie: You too. Make good choices, but
make them naughty too.

Diana: Don't worry, I learn from the best
winking face emoji

16

Jasper

"Are you comfortable being squished in the middle?" I ask Natalie, tucked between Cole and myself on the bench seat of the sleigh. We're ready to set off for the first village and I've never been this excited for a trip. This has the potential to be life-changing, but despite the weight of that thought, I feel light as a feather doing it with Cole and Natalie.

"You know I love being the filling in this monster sandwich," Natalie says and does a little shoulder shimmy.

Just to be sure everyone's good and ready, I tuck the blankets in a little tighter across their laps. Nick had thought of everything, including a stack of the fluffiest of blankets stored in the compartment under the seat that now holds our luggage.

Cole indulges me as I fuss over him, arranging his scarf so it covers his neck, and pulling down his beanie so it covers his pointed ears.

"Don't want these ears to catch frostbite. I want to nibble on them later," I say with a wink. Cole's only reply is a warm smile and slight arch of his brows.

I follow the same procedure with Natalie, making sure she's warm in her new coat, hat, scarf, and gloves, since humans are more susceptible to the cold than us.

"You know I love the cold, right?" Natalie asks.

I frown. "But you were complaining when you got here."

"Well, I was dressed for a tropical summer, except for your sweater you lent me. I get where the misunderstanding comes in, but I've always liked winter more. Besides, I have a bit of an ice kink too," Natalie states with a saucy grin, causing me to choke on my own spit.

I glance around the clearing in front of Cole's house, trying to think how I can make this ride more interesting but coming up empty. "You can't say things like that when we're about to set off on a trip. I want to play now."

Natalie shrugs. "Be a good boy and maybe I'll let you play tonight."

Cole leans forward and pushes me back into the seat. "Keep your cock in your pants. I have plans for you two. Don't think I didn't overhear what you told Natalie earlier about where she's getting stuffed tonight. But behave until then. Think you can do that, Jasper? Natalie?"

I'm so glad Cole included Natalie in that sentence too, that I don't mind being put in place. I fake a pout. "I think I can be good." And just to push his buttons, I add, "Daddy."

Natalie gasps and her eyes turn to saucers, but Cole only huffs a laugh. "Not my kink. But nice try."

"Oh, before we go, um…" Natalie looks nervous and a faint color blooms across her cheeks. "I found this beanie in the clothes Cole got me, so I don't know if this will fit, but I tried to cut holes in it for your horns. Obviously it's not perfect, but…" She trails off and takes out a green-and-white patterned beanie with a giant pom-pom. "You don't have to wear it, but I don't want you to be cold."

Completely unbidden, tears fill my eyes at the sweet gesture.

I take the beanie from her and hug it to my chest. "I love it, thank you." My voice comes out hoarse with emotion and I press my lips together to stop the quiver. "Can you help me put it on?"

Natalie nods and I lean down so she can thread my horns through the beanie, pulling it snug over my ears. There's a similar emotion in her eyes too, one she doesn't try to blink away for a change.

"You look dashing," she says and flicks the pom-pom.

"Thank you, truly. It's my first ever hat." My statement lands in the space between us, ringing in the silence as it sinks in how significant this is for me.

"I'm glad I got to give it to you," Natalie says softly.

Needing to restore to my normal factory settings, I counter with, "I know what else you like to give to me." Natalie's laugh is so sudden and loud that the reindeer turn to look back at us.

"That's our sign. Let's be off," Cole says and grabs the reins. "On Merry, on Jolly."

The sleigh jolts forward as the reindeer start pulling, and it quickly smooths into a glide across the packed snow. I reach for Natalie's hand under the blanket and draw it into my lap, lean back, and just enjoy the ride.

We're silent as we settle in, taking in the sights of the snow-covered trees lining the smooth, well-kept road that transports all the toys the villages make to the central warehouse in Joulu.

The whoosh of the sleigh across the tightly packed snow and the clopping of the reindeer's hooves accompany us, along with the faint ringing of jingle bells coming from the reindeer harnesses.

"By the way," Natalie says, turning to me, "you never told us what Adelbert said over the phone. Anything significant?"

"Ah, yes. He was happy I told him what happened. Apparently, Cole isn't the only one to get a matching tattoo after the island."

"Really? Who?" Natalie asks, tilting her head to look up at me. Cole glances at me over Natalie's head, keeping only a loose hold on the reins since the reindeer don't need much guidance, seemingly well-acquainted with this road.

"He said he's not going into detail on the phone, but from his clues, I'm guessing it's Rollo's brothers who also got bonded to Diana." I can't remember their names, but I do know his older brother is some kind of pack alpha up in Alaska.

"Brothers? How many?" Cole asks.

"Rollo has two brothers. So Diana has three bonded to her now."

"Little minx," Natalie says affectionately. "She's been holding out on me."

"Adelbert's scheduled a video call for tonight, said he has finally figured it out, but wants to tell us as a group. Everyone from the island, plus the newly added tattoo partners will be in on the call," I explain, knowing Bertie would hate to tell the same story multiple times. Poor male must've been under so much stress figuring this out while I've been having the time of my life.

Not like I will say it to his face, but I'm sorry that I'm not sorry. Having Natalie with us has been pretty magical.

"So it's okay for me to sit in on the call too?" Cole asks, brows scrunched together in an oddly nervous manner.

"Of course. Bertie expects you to. You're in this just as much as we are," I say and reach over to squeeze his thigh.

I take out the bag of snacks I prepared, because what's a road trip without snacks, and offer some to Natalie. "How about some sugar plums?"

Natalie throws her head back, her laughter ringing

through the air, and Cole just shakes his head with an amused smile at my choice of snacks.

Plopping one into her mouth, Natalie says, "You know I'll never turn down some sugar plums." She nudges Cole with her shoulder and he leans down to give her a kiss on top of her head. I throw my arm around her shoulder and rest my hand on the back of Cole's neck. This is cozy. I will never get enough of this.

"Hold up," Natalie says and quirks her head at Cole. "Is that why you pretended you were out of gingerbread cream when I was making coffee for Nick."

Cole winces slightly but doesn't deny it. "I'm a little possessive when it comes to that particular flavor. Nick is nice, but not nice enough to share that with him."

"But you shared it with me?"

"Because I share Jasper with you. You're the exception." Cole's blunt honesty hits me like a delicious sucker punch to my solar plexus. The statement has me nearly breathless, sparking anticipation and, dare I say, hope for a real future for the three of us.

We fall into comfortable silence again, letting Cole's words really sink in. The words warm me from the inside like the heat from a fire after a long day out in the cold.

As we draw closer to Puutyöt, my nerves start scratching me. "Cole, do you maybe know if Nick called ahead so they're expecting our arrival?" I hate how shaky my voice sounds, giving away just how much I dread the elves' reactions.

The look Cole gives me is full of understanding, but Natalie's confused gaze flits between us. "What am I missing?"

I take a deep breath before revealing my shame. "Remember how I told you a krampus is considered the bad part about Christmas?" Natalie nods and grips my hand a little tighter before I forge ahead. "Well, the Christmas elves are kind of uncomfortable around me. They're the good guys and I'm the bad guy. When they're not mentally prepared to see me, they literally scream and run away." I gasp when I realize something else. "Fuck. I forgot my glamour ring at the house. Cole, can we go back?"

Cole shakes his head, his eyes full of empathy. "I left it there on purpose. I'm not ashamed of you. Neither is Natalie. If the other elves can't see you for the good male you are, then that's their loss."

Natalie's brows furrow as she considers my words. "So what you're saying is you're nervous about their reactions if you show up and they didn't expect to see you?"

I nod and swallow around a sudden lump in my throat. "Yeah."

Suddenly, Natalie perks up, her eyes sparkling with glee. "I have an idea."

17

Cole

It's been a long time since I've visited Puutyöt and it's even more gorgeous than I remember with its wooden houses, and numerous golden lights adorning the trees.

As evening draws closer and the chill starts to creep in despite all our layers, the reindeer take us through the village toward the guest cottage that Nick usually stays at when he comes here.

Next to me, Jasper and Natalie are stunned silent as they gape at the charming houses. Thick layers of snow cover the wooden A-frames lining the streets. The intricate trim designs along the roofs and the beautifully carved front doors show off the superb craftsmanship of the village carpenters as light spills from windows, casting a golden glow across the pink snowy streets.

The sleigh whooshes to a stop in front of the charming guest cottage, and we sit still for a moment to take in the view. Twinkling lights are strung along the eaves of the sharply sloped roof, and in the glistening pine trees dwarfing the property are ribbons of red and clusters of ornaments scattered between more golden lights. It looks like something from a Christmas greeting card humans send to each other.

Opening the front door is a portly elf waiting for us with palms gently resting on his protruding belly. His affable charm, visible even from here, puts me at ease and I get out to greet him while Natalie and Jasper stay put, eyes still aglow with wonder even if a bit of wariness licks at the corners of their mouths.

I walk up the three front steps and remove my glove to shake the elf's hand. "Good evening. I'm Cole. Thank you for allowing us to stay here." At a little more than a foot shorter than me, the elf is taller than most Christmas elves who rarely reach more than four feet in height. He has tufts of gray hair peeking out from under a red hat with a fluffy trim, dark eyes, a button nose, and quite an impressive long gray beard.

He smiles up at me, the corners of his eyes crinkling as he places a warm calloused hand in my larger one. "Of course, Cole. You're always welcome here. You can call me Tinker, all the elves do." His instant kindness takes me aback, because I've never exactly felt welcome here, or in most places.

I have to take time at some point to reflect if that's because *they* don't want me around, or have I seen everything through a lens of rejection due to my personal baggage?

"Thank you." The surprise must be evident in my voice because Tinker's smile fills with even more warmth like he understands more than what I'm saying.

He places his other hand on top of mine he's still holding. "This might not be my place to say, but you are also one of us. I know we might not share all physical similarities because you have inherited a bit of your father's height," he says with a soft smile, "but you are still a Christmas elf. Now, before your friends freeze their butts to that sleigh, come inside and get warmed up by the fire."

I motion for Jasper and Natalie to join us and a grin splits my face as I take in Jasper's new look. I chance a glance at Tinker to see his reaction to Jasper, but he holds the same friendly expression, with perhaps a bit of amusement dancing in his eyes as they walk up to us, hand in hand.

Jasper ducks his head in an effort to make himself smaller, making the jingle bells attached to his horns shake with the movement.

On the way here, Natalie had the brilliant idea of taking some of the bells from Merry and Jolly's harnesses and attaching them to Jasper's horns. She reckoned that if the elves can hear him coming, they won't be as surprised to see him. And if someone truly had some ill intent toward others, surely they wouldn't wear something as happy as bells. A side effect is that Jasper looks so cute I want to take a bite out of him.

I can't help but think of ways I'm going to move his body to get maximum sound effects from him tonight.

"Well now, that's creative," Tinker says, gesturing to Jasper's bells. "I'm Tinker." The fact that he introduced himself in the same jovial manner, despite them not being elves, has gratitude blooming in my chest.

"Hi, Tinker. I'm Jasper and this is Natalie." Natalie holds her shoulders stiff, still defensive of Jasper. I try to reassure her by taking her other hand and rubbing my thumb across her knuckles. The way her shoulders visibly relax with this small sign of affection from me solidifies how hard I'm going to continue to work to make her mine, *ours*.

Tinker glances at the three of us holding hands but his smile never falters. "Let's get you settled. I can smell fresh snow coming and I can imagine you'd want to be warm and dry after your journey. My grandsons will take care of Merry and Jolly."

At that statement, two young boys in bright green jackets peer around the corner of the house and give us a hesitant wave before approaching the reindeer with treats.

"Are those the reindeer-friendly candy canes?" Natalie asks, rising onto her toes to watch the boys.

"Of course. Now don't you worry, Miss Natalie, we only give them the best of everything. Their stables might even be better than my grandsons' bedrooms. Perhaps if they cleaned their own rooms as well as they prepared the stables, it would be easier to make the comparison. Alas, one cannot have all the luck. Now let's get you warmed up. The boys will bring your bags in shortly after they've finished fawning over the reindeer."

Tinker shuffles into the cottage and we follow close, kicking off our shoes at the door and hanging our coats on the hooks. The living room is clearly designed with a Santa's size in mind, the cream-colored couches made to accommodate frames much larger than elves'.

At the center of the room a fire crackles in the hearth, little hand-carved wooden nutcrackers lining the stone mantel. A plush white rug covers the timber floors in front of it, and images of lying down right there with Natalie and Jasper take center stage in my mind.

Tinker shows us to the snug bedroom. Taking up most of the room is a red-and-white double bed, decorated with heaps of throw pillows and numerous plush blankets. Golden Christmas lights are draped across the carved headboard that, if it was in my house, I'd totally tie Jasper or Natalie to.

Looking slightly embarrassed, Tinker scratches at a spot under his hat. "I apologize for the size of the bed. It has been many years since we've had more than a single guest staying here. Nick usually visits alone, and your father... Well, it might be a bit cramped for the three of you."

Jasper, now clearly comfortable with Tinker, places a hand on the elf's shoulder and I can't help but marvel at how large he looks next to him. "Thanks, Tinker. Cramped is just what we like."

"Or *'krampus,'*" Natalie mumbles. I fold my lips between my teeth to stop my laugh from escaping, not wanting to make this more awkward than it already is.

"That's great, Mister Jasper," Tinker says, obviously catching the meaning but remaining poised. "The fridge and pantry are full, and the missus sent over a cooked meal that's currently warming in the oven. She thought you might be hungry and tired, and didn't want you worrying about anything else." My heart is going to burst out of my chest if this male keeps talking. Never in my life have I experienced anything like this and I'm almost nervous to get used to it.

Seemingly unaware of my current mental crisis as I make sense of this new reality I find myself in, Tinker continues, "The workshop we'd love for you to visit is just down the road and to your right. Can't miss it. We look forward to seeing the three of you in the morning." Looking to Jasper, Tinker adds, "Bells or no bells, you're all welcome." He winks and then he's waving at us over his shoulder as he closes the door.

"Good night," the three of us call after him.

Natalie walks into the kitchen, mumbling either to herself or to us, "And you two said the elves don't like you. If this is what we can expect on this trip then I think it's fair to say you two should reassess what you thought you knew about them. He was maybe one of the nicest people I've ever had the pleasure of meeting." She peers into the oven and takes a deep breath. "It's basically Christmas dinner," she sighs happily. "Roast chicken, mashed potatoes, and green bean casserole. I must be living in a fairy tale. Someone pinch me. Or don't. If this isn't real then I don't want to wake up."

Jasper sweeps her into his arms and leans his forehead against hers. "This is real. So real." And I know he means that in more ways than one. I do too.

I have no idea how my life has changed so quickly in the span of a few days. Maybe Nick called the elves and had a chat with them about me. Maybe Natalie was the catalyst who set it all off. I'm not sure what or how it happened, and I don't particularly want to examine it too closely either. I just want to be happy. And this right here, with them, is happiness.

Jasper holds out a hand and I step into their embrace just as the first pink snowflakes make their leisurely descent out the window.

Bertie: The video call will commence in two hours. Please refrain from being late.

Jamie: I'll see if I can fit it into my schedule *winking face emoji*

Everett: We'll be on time. Sadie and I have stuff to share.

Jasper: Oh, fun! Us too! And you guys get to meet Cole now! *Beaming face emoji*

Edmond: Thank you for setting this up, Bertie.

Harvey: Looking forward to it.

Rollo: My brothers will be joining us too.

Daehan: We will also be in attendance.

Erik: Got it.

Sawyer: *thumbs up emoji*

18

Natalie

After dinner, I move over to the couch to set up the video call with everyone from the island. My heart is in my throat, beating wildly with nerves about whatever Adelbert is going to say.

I'm not even sure what I want the news to be. If he tells us he found a way to dissolve the bond, would the guys want me to leave? Do *I* want to leave?

Originally, I told myself not to catch feelings, and I told myself not to get attached, but I think it's far too late for that now. All my heart flutters are telling me we're past the point of it being "just sex."

Cole and Jasper have me. If they want me. But I think… I think I'm willing to really give things a shot between us.

The males position themselves on either side of me and I turn on the camera to test the angle. "I think you'll have to scooch closer, we don't all fit."

Jasper grips me around my waist and lifts me into his lap. "You know I can always make it fit," he says in a low voice thick with lust that has my pussy gushing.

Cole's eyes heat as he takes us in. "This call needs to be

quick. I can't wait to get my hands on you two." He emphasizes his point by stroking up my thigh, his touch searing my skin through my tights. He shifts his other hand and cups Jasper's cock through his sweatpants, playing with him until we're both breathing heavily.

The call comes through and Cole clicks "join" while Jasper and I try to compose ourselves.

Ten small boxes pop up on the screen and I instantly find Diana, grinning and wiggling my eyebrows at her and holding up three fingers.

She winks back at me and makes a peace sign, indicating my two males a little more subtly.

Adelbert greets the group. "Good day, my brethren and your partners." Not to be dismissive of him, but I imagine he's going to explain things in a very formal manner, so I tune him out and study each box's occupants, trusting the guys to focus on the call and tell me if I miss anything important.

I note Sadie where she's also sitting on Everett's lap. Oh, with those flushed cheeks and that amount of squirming she's trying not to do, I'm sure she's getting finger banged under the table.

Good for you, girl. Make that male multitask with a straight face.

Cole gasps and Jasper's hands tighten around my waist, causing me to tune into the conversation again. "A fated bond is brought on by the stars aligning to bring two, or more, people together. The fates choose the partners and orchestrate the events leading to their meeting," Adelbert explains as if reading from a textbook.

Clearly I've missed something important. *Is a fated bond what we have?*

The others on screen start asking questions, but Cole and Jasper remain silent—stunned, I realize.

I move Jasper's hand from my waist to my thigh, tracing a gentle pattern across it, then reach for Cole with my other hand in a silent show of support to whatever is going on. My touch seems to relax them and Cole gives me a half smile but his focus remains on whatever is being said.

Adelbert continues, "The fated bond causes forced proximity, but it still gives you the choice of getting to know your partner. According to the lore I found, this is a rare occurrence, only to appear about once every thousand years, depending on if the fates deem it necessary."

"Ah, Bertie, you saying we're special?" Jasper jokes, but I sense the tension lying underneath the casual comment as his fingers flex slightly against my waist.

"That's precisely what I'm saying, Jasper," Adelbert says sternly. "Can I continue, or does anyone else have a joke to make?" By the way he's tugging at his hair, Adelbert is extremely stressed about sharing his findings with us, but there's no need to be short with someone who uses humor as a coping mechanism.

I'm about to give him a piece of my mind, but Cole's hand tightens on mine and he gives a subtle shake of his head, clearly reading my intention.

I study Cole's profile as he focuses on the screen. His neck has the most beautiful holly tattoo and tonight I want to give it a lot of attention. Maybe trace the leaves with my tongue and swirl it around the berries. I want to count each piercing in those pointed ears with my teeth, nibble around them, until Cole is quivering underneath me, begging me to fuck him.

Cole snaps me out of my daydreams when he cocks his head as if to hear Adelbert better. "If you make physical contact with your partner, the bond will grow stronger. I believe the *urge* to be close to your partner becomes intense and perhaps even uncomfortable, so please proceed with caution."

Is this why we can't keep our hands off each other? Because once we touch we keep wanting to touch more and more? Makes sense, because I literally can't go five minutes without wanting to be with one of them. But it also begs the question if it's just the bond pushing us together or if they like me enough to *want* to be with me.

Adelbert answers my silent question when he explains, "If you *choose to* pursue the relationship, grow genuine feelings for each other, and make a conscious *choice* to be together, then the fated bond becomes a mate bond."

Behind me, Jasper whispers, "A mate bond." It's so soft, I don't think I was meant to hear it.

I know I must be missing the gravity of what this means because both males' hands grow clammy in mine, and their chests rise and fall much more rapidly than they normally do. Cole looks pale, but the smallest hint of a smile tugs at his mouth. Can't be all bad, then.

Everett, a dhampir, speaks next, explaining more about his bond with Sadie—who is looking more and more flushed by the minute. "This is just to say that some of my more *primal* urges come out with Sadie. I don't know what that would be like for each of your species. Just thought it would be good to be made aware of it."

Primal? Color me intrigued.

Over my shoulder, I study Jasper's face, his ever-present grin that tips his lips up, and the laugh lines around his eyes. His lighthearted chuckle usually sits right below the surface, ready to be released, but he's quiet now as he listens to what the males are saying.

What would a primal Jasper look like? Would he go full krampus on me? The thought has a shudder of desire racing down my spine and my nipples forming into hard points.

Sensing the conference call is coming to an end, I concentrate on Adelbert's final remarks, Florence sitting demurely next to him. "To summarize: you've got a fated bond with forced proximity, it can intensify with touch, it can dissolve over time, or it can strengthen into a mate bond if you choose it to be so."

One by one, people say their goodbyes and Adelbert ends the call. I lean forward to turn the device off and we're plunged into a thick silence.

I shift on Jasper's lap so I can see both of them. Cole's eyes are glassy and Jasper's bottom lip quivers, their gazes flitting between each other and me.

"You're my mates," Jasper states reverently. "I'm in. All in."

"Me too," Cole chokes out, voice thick with emotion.

My heart beats wildly at the emotional proclamation, and I feel awful for having missed exactly what this means. Not wanting to take away from the moment, but needing to be honest, I say hesitantly, "Um, you guys are going to have to explain what 'mates' means. I'm guessing it's not just close friends."

Jasper snorts, the emotional moment broken, and shakes with laughter. He bands an arm around my waist and pulls me flush to him.

Cole cups my face and traces his thumb along my cheekbone, one hand gripping Jasper's. "It means you're ours and we're yours. We were made for each other and the fates brought us together in a very rare, miraculous way."

I don't know whose fist it is, but one squeezes tightly around my heart, a feeling of belonging seeping into my very bones. Heart flutters, stomach flutters, they're all there as Cole's words shatter the last walls that I have erected around my heart. I lean into their truth, letting their meaning sink into the deepest part of my being.

Everything about us has been different, magical. I've

never felt anything like it before, not even imagined having this kind of connection with anyone, let alone two people. It's not something you turn your back on and walk away from.

This connection is real. Raw. True.

Not yet knowing I'm ready to commit to them, Jasper adds, "But it also means you have a choice. If you don't want to be with us then the bond will eventually go away and you can leave." His voice turns almost pleading. "Please just take a moment to consider before deciding."

I narrow my eyes, keeping my face as passive as I can while my heart rampages in my chest. "So you're both in?" I ask. "With each other?"

"Yes." The answer is immediate, confident, unanimous.

"And with me?" I ask to confirm, ready to let go of the last thread holding me back from fully diving into this relationship.

Cole swallows hard, his face etched with earnestness. "If you want us or not, our feelings don't change. We want you."

"We love you." Jasper's voice cracks on the last word, just as the final bricks around my heart tumble down.

"Well, thank fuck because I don't know what to do with all these feelings. I'm pretty sure I love you too. So, sign me up. I'm in!"

Cole tackles me into Jasper and rains kisses down on both of us until we're a tangle of limbs on the floor.

19

Jasper

Is this real life or am I living in one of my many fantasies?

I have mates. Fated mates. It's something whispered about in monster conversations, a myth we can only dream about. The thought that it's real and that Cole and Natalie are mine, feels like hot chocolate and freshly whipped cream spreading out from my heart, the deliciousness warming me from the inside out.

We're on the floor in front of the crackling fireplace, having fallen off the couch when Cole surged over us with his kisses, and love. I've tucked Natalie into my side, Cole straddling my left thigh and Natalie's right thigh as he hovers over us.

Framing my face in his hands, Cole stares deeply into my eyes when he says, "Jasper. I love you. I've loved you for a very, very long time. I—"

"I love you too," I say, interrupting what I'm sure is going to be a very nice speech, but the words burn on my tongue, needing to be said out loud.

Cole's lips crash against mine with so much pent-up

emotion, it robs me of breath. He sucks my tongue into his mouth, dominating our kiss, and I sink into it, sink into him. I pull Natalie tighter into my side as Cole lowers his body down on us, needing to be closer, and I grind against him, his cock hard against mine.

Before I lose my train of thought, I break away from the kiss. Our lips remain close, our breaths mingling. "I've loved you since day one. I know we've never talked about it exactly, but I want more with you. I want everything with you."

Cole's face transforms to one of pure bliss as his lips stretch into a brilliant smile. "Me too. Stay with me." He weaves his free hand into Natalie's hair and looks at her. "Both of you."

Natalie's eyes are wide, brimming with affection and need. She bites her lip and nods. "Okay," she whispers, and the word stamps onto my heart, sealing the final part of my soul.

Unable to resist any longer, I turn my head and place a firm kiss on her lips. "I know this is really fast, but it all makes sense if we're fated mates."

Cole gently traces his thumb across Natalie's cheek and asks, "Little vixen, do you know what that means? Have you heard of fated mates before?"

She shakes her head, and I close my eyes, telling my heart to slow down. I want Natalie to understand what she's signing up for. When, *if*, she chooses us, she needs to do so knowing all the facts.

I sit up and drag her into my lap, wrapping her legs around me as I explain, "It means we were made for each other. Think of it like soul mates. Real soul mates. Two souls, or in our case three, that are each pieces of one whole—and the fates have brought them all together. We fit. It's super rare, like mythical-levels rare, and to have it not only between two people, but three… It's like a fantasy."

Natalie is silent as she listens, her brow furrowed as she catalogs each word. After a couple of seconds, she tilts her head and asks, "So it's a magical meet-cute?"

Cole smiles, but there's a trace of sadness pulling at his mouth. "It's a bit more than that. If you choose to be mated to us, it's a lifelong commitment. An unbreakable bond."

"Oh. That's… intense," Natalie says, her pulse visibly galloping at the base of her neck. "I like you. A lot. Like, *a lot a lot* to the point that it's love. And I want to be with you. But can we maybe date first before jumping into something sounding pretty much like marriage?"

"I think that's good," Cole says. His throat works on a swallow before he continues, "I'm bound to the Arctic Circle. That's quite a lifestyle change to consider, and I want you to be sure before you commit. You just left Arizona, wanting adventures and to gallivant across the world. I'd hate for you to have feelings of regret later if you didn't have the opportunity to explore to your heart's content like you planned."

Despite not wanting to freak her out more, I decide to give her more information about what it would mean to be mated to a krampus. "So, um… krampuses also have their own eccentricities you might need to consider."

Natalie pulls back from our touch and crosses her arms over her chest. "It's starting to sound like you're trying to talk me out of staying."

I grab her shoulders and lower my face until we're eye level. "Fuck no. We want you to stay. But we love you enough to make it *your* choice."

Cole gets on his knees and gently pries her hands free, lacing their fingers. "Your heart, your choice. We're all in with you, but we know the weight of those words and the commitment that will come with them. This bond was fated to bring the three of us together in perfect harmony. If it's not all three of us, it's none of us."

Natalie's cheeks brighten to a beautiful crimson color. Her smile is soft, and she looks anywhere but directly at either of us. Shyly, she says, "How can we be sure this is love if we've only known each other for such a short time?"

I place a finger under her chin and tilt her head up until she's looking directly at me. "It's the fated bond. It speeds things up."

"Magic, huh? That makes sense, I guess. Everything about this trip, about you both… it's been magical." Tucking some strands behind my ear, Natalie prompts gently, "Tell me about the krampus stuff."

"So, remember I told you about my parents living together in the Alps? Well, once they were mated, they basically removed themselves from society because they felt like they didn't need anyone besides each other. Their bond is so strong and they're not even fated mates. Also, there's the mating bite."

"Bite?" Trust Natalie to focus on the part she'd think is kinky. "Like a vampire bite?"

Completely unbidden, the desire to bite her becomes so strong that I lean forward to graze my teeth up her throat, nipping at her ear. There's no mating intention behind the nip, so it doesn't mean anything, but the urge is right beneath the surface.

Somehow sensing I need backup, Cole lifts my sweater and runs his hand up and down my back. The touch grounds me and I rest one hand on his thigh before continuing with my explanation.

"It's usually somewhere on the body, depending on personal preferences. It links you to your mate. Once bitten, you can sense each other through a bond. Depending on the strength of the bond you can sense emotions and even communicate. My parents can have whole telepathic conversations with each other."

Natalie's eyes round and she sits up straighter. "Ooo, tele-pathic conversations? That's really cool. I want that."

My hands tighten on her waist and I will my heart to slow down, to give her the time and space she needs to process it all.

"It's also a soul bond," I say with a controlled smile. "It links my soul to yours and Cole's. It's only broken with death."

Natalie looks at Cole before looking back at me, eyebrows halfway up her forehead. "So the stronger than marriage thing is real, then?"

Cole nods. "Yes, and that's why we want you to take your time. Consider all your options. When you're sure, we'll be waiting."

Natalie turns serious. Her gaze is intent on both of us as she says, "Thank you. I'll try not to keep you waiting too long. Every spare moment I have, I'll be thinking through what life in the Arctic will look like for me, for us."

"Take all the time you need," I say and place a light kiss on her forehead.

Cole tilts his head and adds, "And until then, we'll be courting you. Showing you the benefits of staying." He turns his gaze to me. "And you. I'll be courting my krampus too." Like a snowman on a warm day, I melt at those words.

I love Cole so much and knowing he feels the same way about me, that we have a future together—a real one, not the half relationship we've been having until now—makes my internal smile stretch to one that'll rival the Grinch's.

Needing to switch modes before I'm a puddle of cozy feelings on the floor, I cup Natalie's pussy through her leggings. "Also, until you're absolutely sure, we'll be taking care of your sweet cunt with our utmost devotion."

Natalie grinds against my hand. "Can I take your knot?"

"Turns out, as my fated mate, you're made to take it." The

truth of the sentence has me giddy with the knowledge that I won't hurt her, that her cunt was made to accommodate my knot. My smile grows as I realize that Cole, as my other mate, might also be able to take me one day.

I press the heel of my hand harder against Natalie's clit, and she grinds against it until she's breathless. "Is this why I'm constantly dripping?" she pants.

"It's not just arousal, it's slick. It's because your body is preparing to take a krampus cock. And my knot."

Cole's hand moves from my back to my belt, and undoes my pants. My hard cock springs free and he slowly toys with it. He drags his thumb down my slit, gathering precum to lick from his fingers.

Natalie watches us, her breaths growing more rapid as she rides my hand hard. "Can we try it? Knotting?"

Abruptly, I take my hand away, stopping her orgasm before it crests. "Hop on."

20

Jasper

I make quick work of Natalie's clothes, my own somehow dissolving away as Natalie and Cole's hands move up and down my body, distracting me with tongues and teeth, nibbling and licking at each inch of skin revealed.

I find myself splayed out on my back in front of the fireplace, Natalie straddling my waist and Cole's hands cupping her full tits from behind, plucking at her nipples until she's a squirming mess and I can feel her wet cunt hot against my bare skin.

Cole turns Natalie's head and licks into her mouth with a filthy kiss before pulling back abruptly. "Get that cock in your cunt, Natalie. I'll be back."

I try to watch him go, confused as to what's happening and how he's still dressed, but my aching cock and the naked woman on top of me distracts me.

"You heard the male." Natalie's husky voice has my cock twitching. Her smirk is confident as she braces her palms on my chest, lifts her hips and positions me at her entrance, nudging my tip in.

I suck in a breath and grip her thighs, my fingers pressing into her skin as I hold her still. The kiss of her wet heat wrapping around my tip has me starving for more, my chest rising and falling, trying to control myself.

"Go slow, please. I know how well you can take me, but please don't hurt yourself," I grit out.

Natalie's smirk softens for a fraction of a second before turning playful. "You just lie back like a good boy and let me take care of your cock. Okay, puppy?"

"Puppy? I'd like to think I'm more of an alpha."

"Prove it."

I flip us and pin Natalie under me, capturing her wrists with my right hand. I pinch her left nipple and ask, "Who's the puppy now?"

The moan from her is delicious and I thrust my hips lightly, sinking in another inch. "That's it. Spread these legs for me. Let me get nice and deep. I want to see your stomach bulging with my cock."

Panting, Natalie squirms on my cock until I slide in halfway. I rub gentle circles around her clit, giving her a moment to adjust as I watch a beautiful flush spread across her cheeks, down her neck, tinting even her chest.

Out of the corner of my eye, I note Cole entering the room again, carrying all the blankets from the bed and dropping them in a heap next to us. "I like the idea of fucking on a hard floor, but someone's going to end up bruised if we don't cushion it a little."

"I just— I can't—" Natalie stammers. "Please, more."

Feeling particularly naughty, I pull out an inch. "You're the one who said you like edging, right?"

Natalie growls at me and tries to wriggle herself onto my cock. In a very good imitation of Cole's voice, I tut at her, "Now that's not the behavior of a good girl, is it?"

Whack!

I hear the sound before I register the pain of Cole's hand on my ass, my hips reflexively thrusting forward, trying to escape another slap. Natalie clamps around me, holding almost my entire length hostage in her tight cunt.

Behind me, Cole chuckles. "This is fun." Before I have time to protest, he says, "Jasper, pull out. Both of you get over here."

The pure disbelief in Natalie's eyes amuses me. There's a rebellious spirit burning behind those icy irises, ready to argue with Cole.

I shake my head at her. "There's no use. Cole will always get his way. And his way is usually much more fun."

With a wink, I pull out and release her wrists. She whimpers at the loss of me, my own mouth pulling down in a frown when my cock is out of her warm cunt.

Looking down between us, I study Natalie's arousal coating my cock, and can't help but be fascinated by it. I run a finger along my length and pop some sugar cookie slick into my mouth. My eyes roll back in my head as my tongue wraps around my finger, her flavor dancing along my taste buds.

Pulling my finger from my mouth, I groan, "It's impossible to ever get tired of this flavor."

I pull Natalie into a seated position and Cole watches us with a nearly feral glint in his eyes. "Crawl to me."

A breath shudders out of me and Natalie visibly trembles. Neither of us argue. Instead, as if Cole is pulling some kind of magical puppet strings, the two of us crawl across the blankets and kneel at his feet.

Cole, too, falls to his knees and pulls us in for a three-way kiss. His hand wraps around my cock, and the wet sound of his fingers entering Natalie's pussy has my eyes flying open. He plays with us until we're both messy, precum and slick dripping down our thighs and onto the blankets.

My heart hammers in my chest, anticipation building for what Cole has planned next. His hand pauses and a desperate whine crawls up my throat.

"Jasper, bend over, please. Show us that tight ass." The thought of protesting doesn't even make it into my head before my elbows are on the ground and my ass is in the air.

I can't see them, but I hear shuffling and whispering right behind me. My teeth sink into my lower lip to contain the whimpers that want to escape, but a groan is ripped from my throat when a hot tongue licks against my hole.

"Fuuuuuuck," I stutter out, my breath sawing in and out of my lungs as a second tongue joins the first.

Cole and Natalie lick me, rim me, fuck me with their tongues until a steady stream of precum drips from my cock. Their hands are all over me, fondling my balls, stroking up my back, but never touching my cock.

The sounds of them enjoying themselves, their moans and groans as they feast on me, sets my body on fire.

As if sensing I'm close, they pull back at the same time and I collapse onto my back, my pulse running rampant through my body. "Fuck. Double torture."

"Too much?" Natalie asks, concern lacing her words.

"No," I say with a pout. "I, too, perhaps enjoy some edging."

Cole kneels next to me and runs a hand through my hair. "You did so good for us." I lean into his touch, but I'm too worked up for gentle praise right now.

Shifting my gaze to Natalie, I ask, "You ready for both of us?"

"You bet your ass I am," Natalie drawls.

I get up instantly and they help me rearrange the blankets until they're the perfect distance from the fire. I lie down in the middle and fist my cock. "Sit your sweet cunt on my fat cock, Natalie."

"It'll be my pleasure."

Just as before, I let her work her way down, encouraging her while circling her clit with my thumb. Behind her, I watch Cole undress, my mouth watering with each inch of inked skin revealed. He gets rid of his tight T-shirt, then his cock springs free as he pulls his pants and underwear off in one move.

Like he knows where my mind is, he arches a single brow at me and moves his hand up and down his cock, reminding me of how good he feels when he fucks me with long, hard strokes.

Cole positions himself next to Natalie and turns her face to him. "Open," he says, the word straddling the line between demand and request.

At the slightest parting of lips, Cole pushes his cock forward, pushing and pushing, until her lips are pressed against the wide base, her throat full of his cock. She relaxes into it and unconsciously sinks down the last couple of inches on my cock until it's fully sheathed.

Cole pulls back out and grins at her. "So easily distracted with a mouth full of cock." He grips her chin between his thumb and forefinger and tilts her face so she's looking at me. "Look how happy you're making Jasper. See the way his pulse is pounding in his throat? You did that." He brings her gaze back to him and places a hard kiss on her lips. "I'll give you one minute for your first orgasm, then I'm going to squeeze into this tight ass so you can feel both your mates inside you. You got that?"

Natalie's eyes are wide, but she nods, seemingly unable to form a snarky sentence.

"Words, Natalie."

"Yes. Got it," she replies breathlessly.

Knowing he means it, I refocus on her clit and say, "Ride me."

It only takes about thirty seconds for Natalie's walls to clamp down on my cock, her cunt trying its best to rip an orgasm from me. Somehow, I keep a grip on myself, delaying my orgasm for a little while longer as her fingers claw at me, seeking purchase while she rides a wave of bliss.

Eyes heavy lidded as she regains herself, Natalie folds forward and drapes herself across my chest. I wrap my arms around her, trailing soft patterns up and down her back as Cole kneels between my thighs.

Cole's fingers skim against my knot and my brows furrow as I try to figure out what he's doing. He gives me a knowing grin before retreating. He repeats the move a couple of times and I realize he's coating his fingers and cock with Natalie's slick.

Natalie moans and clenches around me again, and I tilt her face to kiss her. Our tongues tangle in a lazy kiss, a sensual embrace of chaotic lust.

Cole croons, "Oh, yes. This is such a nice ass, Natalie. You've already taken one finger. Let's stretch you to take another."

She pushes back against Cole's hand, moans into my mouth, and I can't help but take the kiss deeper. Soon, what started as gentle, turns ferocious as our tongues battle with unbridled passion.

Natalie gasps and pulls back from the kiss, her eyes rolling back in her head as Cole positions his cock at her back hole and pushes in, the veins around his cock rubbing against me through the thin barrier separating us.

"That's it, Natalie. The head's in. You're taking both of us so well. You feel so good," Cole praises.

"I can feel you," I rasp out, and move my hands to her ass, holding her still so everyone has a moment to adjust.

"More," Natalie demands, her jaw set and eyes blazing with fierce determination.

Cole pushes in a little more and I huff out a breath. The feel of him rubbing against me is divine. I want to do this every day.

Slowly, we pant our way through Cole's methodical invasion until he leans over Natalie, his whole body flush with hers. He traces the base of my horn with his fingers and I smile up at him, feeling more complete like this than I ever have in my life before.

"This is a sweet moment, but one of you needs to move. I need— I need—"

Cole sucks her earlobe into his mouth and says, "I know exactly what you need."

He pulls out carefully until only the tip remains inside, then thrusts back hard, rocking Natalie deeper on my cock. The bells on my horns jingle with the movement. It almost makes me want to laugh, but the feeling is too incredible to do anything but moan with pleasure.

When he pulls back again, his voice rumbles with possessiveness. "I want you two to lie nice and still while I fuck you. I want to make my mates come, knowing it was me who did this to you."

Then, Cole starts thrusting in earnest. He becomes a master of our bodies, fucking us with complete abandon as he drives us higher and higher with each powerful snap of his hips.

Natalie pushes herself up slightly, bracing her palms next to my head. She throws her head back and closes her eyes as she chases her next orgasm. Her tits bounce in my face and I stick my long tongue out to wrap around a nipple, pulling on it. Her eyes fly open at the sensation and she screams our names as pleasure seizes her body. Goose bumps run up and down her arms and she arches against me, her cunt pulsating around my cock like it knows it belongs to her.

Not yet, I tell myself, clenching my jaw tightly, not wanting this to be over too soon.

Cole must see it as a personal challenge, because he doesn't slow down, just keeps going until Natalie comes again, her slick soaking both of us.

When she settles back into her body, Cole asks me, "You still want to knot her, Jasper?" His breathing is jagged, like he himself is riding the edge. Judging by the strained tendons in his neck and the sweat dotting his skin, I know he's just as close as I am.

"Yes." The word is hardly more than a staccato of breath from my throat.

Natalie echoes my sentiment with a breathy, "Knot me. Please."

"Good. Jasper, you're going to hold off until I'm done. I'm going to pump Natalie's ass full of sugar plum cum before you get to knot her. I want to watch my seed drip down her crack, mingling with your releases. You two got that?"

"Yes." Cole must've fucked the ability to form full sentences out of us.

Cole wraps his hand around Natalie's hair, making her arch back as he picks up the pace, a wild glimmer in his eyes telling me that we're really in for it.

He snaps his hips forward at a rapid pace. Natalie's cries ring through the room. My own harsh breathing echoes in my ears as I watch my two mates fall apart in front of me.

With a growl of, "Mine," Cole comes, emptying himself into Natalie's sweet ass. His release triggers hers, a soundless cry falling from Natalie's smudged cherry-red lips as her orgasm steals her breath, her eyes falling shut as tremors run through her body.

Cole pulls out slowly and Natalie's eyes flutter open. He gives me a single nod and sits back on his heels to watch his cum dripping from her hole, before he collapses back on his elbows, his dazed eyes intent on where we're joined.

Not being able to hold back any longer, I grip Natalie's waist and flip her onto her back. I throw her legs over my shoulders, and then I'm driving into her with rough, inelegant strokes.

The desire to knot someone for the first time in my life overrides my normal senses.

I thumb her clit as sensation builds low in my spine, quickly spreading through my whole body, making my knot swell, signaling my release. I fuck harder into her wet cunt, popping my knot past the ring of muscle that's meant to lock me in.

Natalie's eyes widen, her mouth gapes open, but there's surprise and delight in her eyes as twin orgasms wrack through our bodies, and her cunt seals my knot inside.

The feeling is nothing like I've ever known before. It's not just hitting a peak, it's transcendent.

It's like climbing up the highest mountain and free-falling down the other side, knowing there's a safety net to catch you.

It's the first ray of sun after months of darkness.

It's Cole's kiss after not seeing him for months.

It's finding your fated mates after thinking you might end up alone.

I roll onto my back, draping Natalie over my chest, filling her sweet pussy with more cum than I have ever produced.

I lay my arm out, not having the energy or the mind to form any sentences, and Cole curls into my side. He takes Natalie's limp hand and lays their joint hands on my heart.

"Have I died and gone to heaven?" Natalie croaks out with a wobbly grin.

"Nope," I rasp. "This is what it feels like to be fucked and knotted by your mates."

"If this is what I can expect for any future encounters, where do I have to sign to make things official?"

A choppy laugh comes from Cole. "I think you're cock drunk. After some sleep, we can talk again."

Natalie mumbles, "I think I've had more orgasms since I've met you than I've had this year. And that's a lot."

"Are you challenging us to give you more? Want to be absolutely sure of that estimation?" Cole teases.

Natalie narrows her eyes at him. "I can't tell if you're joking or not. I don't even care right now. I'm so full and so happy. I can stay like this forever."

I trail my fingers along her back, trying not to think about orgasms or any sexual thoughts. If I remain aroused, my knot will remain inflated, especially when it's getting hugged so tightly by her super wet, hot cunt.

"Give it about thirty minutes, then my knot will come down," I say and picture cold snowflakes landing on my skin, anything to get my focus off sexual ideas.

Cole's voice is very suggestive when he says, "And then cleanup will start."

Natalie shakes her head. "I'm a limp fish. I don't think I have the leg power to even walk to the bathroom to clean up."

Smile turning devilish, Cole explains, "Don't worry, we have tongues. We'll put them to good work. You just lie back and let us take care of you."

"Merry Christmas to me."

21

Cole

"**Y**ou ready to go?" I call to Natalie while threading Jasper's horns through his beanie and tucking it snug over his ears. As if my hand has a mind of its own, I reach up and flick one of the bells attached to his horns, reminding myself of how much fun it was last night to make them jingle in other ways.

Natalie saunters into the room looking especially beautiful. She's wearing a tiny black skirt over thick tights I'm intent on not destroying today—the woman needs her warm clothes if she's going to survive in this climate. Her lips match her maroon sweater, and a tiny sliver of skin is visible on her waist. I imagine Jasper and I will make it our personal goal to keep that inch of skin warm all day.

"All done," Natalie says and places a light kiss on my cheek like it's the most natural thing in the world to do. Just as predicted, Jasper's hands find her waist, fingers splaying over the exposed skin as he pulls her back to his front.

I shrug on my black jacket and hand Jasper his coat. "First stop is Tinker's workshop. I'm hoping we find some kind of inspiration for a gift for the Naughty List kids. If you can think of anything, please speak up and we can ask Tinker to help us brainstorm—I think he might enjoy that."

"Paddles won't work, will they?" Natalie jokes as she straightens my jacket, smoothing her hands over my chest.

I reach down and pinch her ass. "Maybe on you, but let's not try that with them."

"Oh, that's giving me ideas," Jasper says and bounces on his feet.

I back them into the door with my hips, sandwiching Natalie just the way she likes. "Let's try to behave today. I don't want to scar any of the elves with our… shenanigans."

Jasper pulls me closer by the collar of my shirt and kisses me like he's got a point to prove. His tongue dominates mine until I'm reaching for him around Natalie, my cock hard against her stomach.

Natalie lets out a contented sigh between us. "I can watch you two all day. Unfortunately—and I can't believe I'm the one to say this—I think it's better if we leave now before we end up naked within the next minute."

Jasper and I pull back, both utterly breathless. He runs his tongue along his teeth and looks me up and down, banding one arm across Natalie's chest. "If we behave today, can we misbehave tonight?"

Natalie tilts her head and flutters her lashes at us. "I've never seen the Eiffel Tower before. Maybe tonight you two can show me?"

I help her into her coat then pull her toward the door, mumbling, "Let's go before we take you right now."

OUR BREATHS MIST the air and our boots crunch against the

snow as we walk through the quiet streets toward the center of the village, following Tinker's directions.

Window displays from bakeries and quaint tea shops compete for our attention. The smells of freshly baked bread, pastries, and other confections entice us to step off the path and satisfy the sweet tooth we all share.

One shop has wooden snowflakes dangling over a miniature Christmas town, fake snow sprinkled across the roofs. Another has a variety of baked goods stacked on ribboned boxes, all framed by garlands of stars and twinkling lights. The grocer's window displays an army of nutcrackers holding samples of vegetables and other products they sell. My stomach grumbles despite our hearty breakfast of bacon, eggs, and sausages that Coco—Tinker's wife—sent over.

It's only through our sheer willpower that we're able to turn the corner and make our way to the wood workshop. The sight before us trumps everything else we've yet seen.

Wordlessly, we come to a halt as we take in the only painted building in town. The exterior walls are pine green, mimicking the large trees flanking the workshop. Giant white snowflakes adorn its facade—each uniquely carved with built-in twinkling lights. Through the paned windows, we can just make out the shape of elves bathed in warm golden light, hard at work to create toys for the children on the Good List.

The rustic-red double doors creak open, and we're greeted by the soft humming of a faintly familiar tune coming from the elves within.

Tinker steps out—a small, patient smile in place as he waits for us to walk closer. "Welcome, dear friends. I hope you had no trouble finding us?"

I'm still scouring my brain for words when Natalie speaks. "I think this might be the most magical place I've seen in my life. Can we please come in?" Her tone is one of awe, her words holding no snark. There's a beautiful honesty in them, almost an innocent wonder as she strains her neck to see more over Tinker's shoulder.

"Of course." Tinker's eyes crinkle in delight. "Follow me." The old male holds out his elbow for Natalie and she easily slips her hand into the crook of his gentlemanly arm. It somehow works despite their height difference, the sight making me wish I can imprint it on my mind.

Jasper quirks a brow at me and sticks his arms out too. I gladly hook my arm through his and we follow them inside.

The entire room is warm, both in temperature and in the reception we get from everyone. Raising their heads from their workbenches, the elves smile, nodding greetings at us before returning to their work, but I sense half of their attention remains trained on us. Their collective humming picks back up and I smile when I realize the song they've unwittingly chosen reflects the Christmas tattoos across my body.

We follow Tinker to the far end of the room, my eyes flitting from one corner to the next, trying to take in every detail I can see.

Exposed wooden beams run along the length of the room. Clusters of red, green, and gold ornaments are strung from the rafters with tiny twinkling lights artfully draped between them.

In one corner is a fireplace keeping the large workshop cozy, nutcrackers standing guard on either side.

Each station has four elves working together on a specific toy. Every team seems to be responsible for a different design. Saws, hammers, chisels, wrenches, pliers, screwdrivers, spanners, and a host of tools I can't name are neatly arranged against the backboard of each workbench.

Along the eastern wall is a wider variety of similar tools, organized by size and type. The western wall has shelves for the different designs currently being built and displays each toy's blueprint next to it. My eyes hop from one toy to the next, not being able to catalog them fast enough.

Tinker comes to a stop in front of the tall wall at the end of the room and my mouth gapes open as I study the samples of toys.

"These are the original toys that Nick made. He designs a prototype and sends it to us for our input. The elves select which toy they'd like to work on, then they try to perfect the design during the first half of the year. Once Nick approves the final design, we place it on the western wall, and focus on multiplying it according to the estimated number of requests Santa will receive for the coming Christmas."

I stare up at the sheer variety of designs Nick has completed. How does he manage it all? And this is only one of the villages. I'm glad he has the elves to help him because this looks like it takes a staggering amount of time to come up with.

There's a wooden teddy bear, a rocking horse, toy train, tractor, dinosaur, doll house, stacking rings, a complete stable with animals. Even a little kitchen.

Natalie takes out her leather-bound sketchbook and says, "Is it okay if I draw some of this? It's so pretty and I don't want to forget one detail of this sight."

"Of course," Tinker replies graciously. "Make yourself at home. Take your time to look around. I'll be at my bench over there if you have any questions."

Natalie opens the sketchbook and flips through it for a blank page. I swear I see something that resembles me, and step closer at the same time Jasper does. He puts a finger between two pages to halt her movement.

"Can I see that?" Jasper is nearly breathless with the question. My heart starts to beat rapidly, like a runaway sleigh is dragging it across a frozen lake as I wait for her answer.

Natalie's eyes dart between us and a shy blush pinkens

her face and neck. "Yeah, but don't judge them too harshly, okay?"

"Never," Jasper says and places a chaste kiss on her forehead before gently prying the book from her hands.

I step closer and wrap an arm around Natalie's waist, peering down at the most exquisite drawing. She captured me so accurately, but in a way I've never seen myself before. I'm in the sleigh, holding the reins in one hand while looking at something—or *someone*—not visible in the picture. But the emotion on my face is one of pure adoration, of love and devotion.

She saw and drew my feelings for Jasper before I had even verbalized the words to him.

"You're so talented," I breathe against her ear, squeezing her closer to me.

Jasper's eyes brim with tears as he pages through her sketchbook, revealing a few scenes from her time in the Caribbean, but mostly details of the North Pole.

She drew the snowcapped trees, the reindeer, the sleigh, three hot chocolate mugs in front of the fire, our feet tangled together on the bed, and then there's the sketch of Jasper.

A shaky breath shudders out of him and he blinks up at the rafters as emotion overwhelms him. A tear rolls down his cheek and I quickly thumb it away before it can fall on the book.

"We need to frame this one," I say after a moment of silently staring at the image. I can feel Natalie's love for Jasper in this single image. The way she views him speaks louder than any words she can say.

It's Jasper with his arms casually crossed over his chest, and a mischievous smirk pulling up the corners of his mouth. She was able to capture the sparkle in his caramel eyes and the majesty of his curved horns. The way she juxtaposed his playfulness with his softness has my heart melting for both of them.

"I know it's not very professional, but—"

I put my finger over her mouth, halting her speech. "Don't you dare say a negative thing right now. I'm in love with these drawings and I can't wait to see more."

Natalie pulls her lips into her mouth, her chest inflating on a big breath, before she says softly, "It's my memory book. I'm not good with fancy words and descriptions, so the images replace what I can't say."

"Natalie. They're amazing. You're amazing," Jasper says and pulls her into a hug.

"I just… I want…" she mumbles against his chest, eyes also getting teary now.

Jasper draws back and frames her face. "Whatever you want, it's yours. But I'm telling you, each of your drawings is a story in itself. They're so inspiring to me that I can imagine a whole story and happy ending for each of them."

My mouth curves up into a smile when the best idea strikes me. "Didn't you say you wanted to become a tattoo apprentice? If you're staying, I can put you in contact with my artist. I would love to have this sketch of Jasper tattooed on me."

Natalie's eyes light up. "Really?"

I nod. "Yeah. And if it's okay with you, I'd like you to draw one of yourself. I want to add you, too."

Blinking rapidly, Natalie pauses before saying with pure shock. "You want to get *me* tattooed on *you*?"

I incline my head in a nod, and tap a finger to her chest to emphasize my point. "And I'd like *you* to do the tattooing. If you're okay with it, of course."

"I— Yeah."

I realize the room has gone silent and, simultaneously, we turn to see what's going on. Wide eyes and grinning open mouths greet us before they all quickly return to work, pretending they weren't watching us.

Tinker joins us again and places a hand on his heart. "Here, we love love, and celebrate it in all its forms. And you three are giving us enough fuel to last until Christmas." In a lower voice he adds, "I'm sorry if that moment was meant to be private, but the elves are very curious to have you here. We don't have these big ears for nothing." He winks at Natalie and she lets out an adorable giggle.

"Now," Tinker continues, "let me walk you through the system, from when we receive Santa's designs until they're finished and sent back to Joulu for packaging and storage."

Cole: Hi Nick. We visited your Puutyöt workshop yesterday. It's really something special.

Nick: Do you think so? The elves are so nice there.

Cole: VERY nice. Especially to me. Did you have something to do with that?

Nick: Not really. Just told them you were coming. Their niceness is all their own.

Nick: Find any inspiration for a replacement?

Cole: Not yet, but it's still early days.

Nick: Make sure you enjoy yourselves too. Have fun and relax.

Cole: Thanks, Nick. Will message when we get to Pehmolelu.

Nick: I look forward to it.

22

Natalie

The next day, we return to the workshop, and the next. We spend a full week in Puutyöt.

We visit with the elves, we learn how to carve toys, learn about how each elf chooses their favorite design. We visit the tea shops, the bakeries, we try all the food, and we fall in love.

Not just with the village and the elves, but with each other. Deeper and deeper, every day.

I thought I was in the North Pole for a good time, an adventure, but I had no idea how life altering it would be.

I am utterly besotted with Jasper and Cole. If I thought we were insatiable before, it is nothing compared to how it is now. Every moment we can, we have our hands all over each other. Early mornings, lunchtime, before dinner, during dinner, all night until we're so tired we just need to sleep.

They explore my ice kink, doing delectable things to my body that I can't wait to repeat. We take turns being in charge. We try every position and combination we can think of. Cole and Jasper have moments with just the two of them, sometimes I watch with a very happy smile, and sometimes I excuse myself to go draw instead.

I also have alone time with Jasper, alone time with Cole, and my connection with them is so all-encompassing, it feels like they're rooted in the very fabric of my being—becoming bonded to my soul.

Being with them is comfortable and exciting at the same time, and the mere thought of walking away from this relationship is unfathomable.

Tomorrow, we say goodbye to Puutyöt and set off for Pehmolelu—the village responsible for making soft toys like stuffed teddy bears. I can't wait to make a mini Jasper and mini Cole teddy.

Walking into the living room, Jasper sets three cups of mulled wine on the coffee table.

"I can't believe our stay here is over." Jasper's bottom lip forms into the most adorable pout as he plops down on the soft rug in front of the fireplace.

Cole picks his cup up but pauses before taking a sip. "Can you believe we've been here for a week?"

I lean back on my side of the couch, stretching my legs into Cole's lap as I wait for my wine to cool down a little. "I'm thinking we should make this a yearly trip. I'd love to visit Tinker and all the Puutyöten elves again."

"Yearly?" Cole quirks an eyebrow, a hint of hope creeping into the seemingly casual question.

"Yearly," I confirm, letting the implication of the statement hang in the air. They've not yet asked me again if I want to stay, giving me the space to make my decision in my own time.

Jasper tries to act like that single word didn't have a strong impact on him, but the way his butt wiggles on the carpet reminds me of a happily wagging tail.

"Do you have a favorite memory from the week?" Jasper asks, eyes wide and expectant.

An irrepressible smile lifts the corners of my mouth. "I have a couple. One in particular was when I was riding Cole reverse cowgirl and you were fucking us with that delicious tongue at the same time."

Cole's eyes glaze over like he's recalling that exact scene. "Honestly, that is a night I never want to erase from my mind. I was always curious how it would feel having a knot. Jasper wrapping his tongue around the base of my cock so I could knot you was mind-blowing. I don't think anything could top that."

Crossing my arms over my chest, I say, "Don't go putting challenges down like that. We might just come up with something even more creative."

Jasper crawls forward and kneels between Cole's legs. Placing his forearms on Cole's knees, he glances at me before back at Cole. "Like the first night we used the paddle?"

Running his hand along Jasper's horn, Cole taps two of the bells that somehow keep increasing, thanks to elves loving Jasper's new look. He currently has six jingle bells of different sizes and colors adorning his horns. The elves no longer fear Jasper—if they ever really did—but view it as a privilege to "beautify" him.

"Poor Tinker." Cole chuckles. "He really indulged us when we made that paddle. I know we were supposed to be focused on the Naughty List, but that paddle was practically begging to be made."

"It's been very useful, hasn't it?" Jasper asks and waggles his eyebrows at me.

"Very," Cole agrees and gives me a lascivious once-over.

Jasper sits up a little straighter, his eyes shining as he asks, "Should we use the paddle tonight?"

I shake my head, not even bothering to consider this

question. "No, my ass still has the imprint of a Christmas tree from two nights ago when you 'punished' *me* for being naughty."

Jasper sits back on his heels, looking a little deflated. "You may have deserved it. I couldn't concentrate on a word Tinker said, knowing you were wearing the anal beads from the first night we met."

I smirk. "Well, it was worth it. Edging myself all day to get double teamed at night was so much fun."

Jasper's voice turns sultry. "You always like being double teamed."

I pick up my cup and hold it out to him in a salute. "So do you."

Cole sits up and reaches for his own mulled wine, tutting playfully at us. "No paddle tonight, you two. Your asses will be too sore in the sleigh tomorrow. It's a couple of hours' ride to Pehmolelu, and I want you to be comfortable."

"Feel like wearing your beads instead?" Jasper asks. The dare in his voice baits me just enough to know I'll say yes.

I pretend I'm considering my answer, and throw my own dare out. "Only if you wear a plug."

Jasper doesn't even hesitate. "Deal." He holds out his hand for me to shake, anticipation dancing in his eyes. I know the same feeling is reflected in mine as I shake his hand.

Cole clears his voice and sets down his now-empty cup. "Not like I want to change the topic, but can you show us your latest sketches? I've been waiting all day to see them."

Jasper jumps up and grabs his cup. "Oh yes. I got a glimpse of one of the drawings and I already have a story drafted for it." Not waiting for a response from me, he chugs his mulled wine and plops back down in front of the couch, resting his back between Cole's spread thighs.

Like every other night since our first visit to the workshop, Jasper pulls me into his lap. Cole runs his hands through Jasper's hair, making the male under me practically purr with contentment. I hand over my sketchbook to Jasper, and he flips through it, finding the right place.

He pages past the wreath door handles of the workshop's front door, past the snowflakes decorating the exterior of the building, past the one I did of Tinker and Coco yesterday. He pauses when he gets to my latest one of the two nutcrackers standing guard next to the fireplace.

"I loved drawing them," I explain, tracing a finger over the one on the left's hat. Those two specific nutcrackers see so much in that workshop, it just felt right to give their eyes a certain alertness.

Clearly inspired by how I portrayed them, Jasper starts his story, Cole and I eagerly hanging on to every word out of his mouth.

Choosing between this being my favorite part of the day, or the sex that will doubtlessly follow after, is almost impossible. It's like trying to choose between Cole and Jasper. They're both perfect in their own way, each providing me with a nourishment my soul really craves. The three of us together is how it's meant to be.

When Jasper finishes his story about the nutcrackers and how they came alive to help save Christmas, I smile up at him. "I think this is your best one yet. I have nothing to add to it."

Cole clears his throat, almost sounding emotional. "That was really touching. It was like I was part of the story. Those nutcrackers are real heroes."

Jasper preens under the compliments. "Thank you. But it's Natalie's drawings that really moved me. I know they're wooden dolls, but there's something magical about the way she captured them."

"Talking about capturing things…" Cole gets up from the couch and returns a moment later. He kneels down in front of me where I'm still in Jasper's lap on the floor. "I noticed your book is almost full."

I page through the five remaining blank pages and swallow hard. "I've been so inspired since I got here. I've never drawn so much so quickly. There are just so many details I don't want to miss."

"You're so talented, and I want you to draw to your heart's content." Cole takes out a wrapped box that looks to be about the size of my current sketchbook, but I rein myself in from jumping to conclusions. He continues, "I hope this isn't too presumptuous of me, but I ordered you a new one from Kirja—the book village we'll get to eventually, but I didn't want you to wait."

He hands over the box, looking adorably nervous. "Thank you, Cole."

"Open it," Jasper encourages and tickles my sides.

"It's not fully done," Cole starts to explain when I reveal the hunter-green sketchbook inside. "I ordered the binding to be in the same color as the books I bound on my shelf, but your name still needs to be foiled. When we get back home I'll finish it there, but I wanted you to have it now."

With tears welling in my eyes, I whisper, "Home."

In that single word, I know this is it.

I try to blink the tears away for a couple of seconds before I let them fall freely. "Jasper, Cole, you are my home. I'm staying. With you. If it's in the Arctic, in the Alps, or in the Sahara—it doesn't matter. *You* are my adventure. My destination."

"You're in? You're fully accepting the bond?" Jasper asks, his grip on my waist tightening with his excitement.

Certainty strengthens my voice. "There was never really a question about it. I just needed time to confirm what I knew to be true. You're my mates and I'm yours."

Cole's eyes mist and he cups my face. "My human mate."

He cups Jasper's face with his other hand. "My krampus mate." Drawing our foreheads together, he whispers, "How did I get so lucky?"

Jasper's voice is thick and wet with emotion. "I didn't even think I was on the fates' radar, and then they go and give me two of you."

I draw back and wipe the mascara from under my eyes. "Before we become blubbering messes, how do we make it official?"

"There's not one specific way, but I can show what I have in mind," Jasper says, his emotion quickly morphing into seduction, the innuendo clear in his suggestion.

"Tell me more," I murmur before slanting my mouth against his.

While we may not have found anything for the Naughty List in Puutyöt, we did learn a lot about toys, as well as each other. There are still plenty of villages to visit, plenty of time to figure out what will be the perfect replacement for coal this Christmas, and I'm doing it with my soul mates.

Natalie: How's life with three males?

Diana: How's life with two males?

Natalie: Guess you're glad we had that anal conversation on the island?

Diana: Maaaaaybe...

Natalie: You tease. Love it for you.

Diana: How's the trip?

Natalie: Eventful. Very, very eventful.

Diana: Details, please.

Natalie: We're still between places, but when we're settled let's have a video chat. I want all YOUR details too.

Diana: Deal.

23

Jasper

The sight that greets us when our sleigh enters Pehmolelu is one that my wildest imagination can't dream up.

"Holy fuck," Natalie whispers, reflecting my exact thoughts.

Fluffy garlands of pine with strings of golden light zigzag across the main street, ribbons of red drawing one's eye to the extravagant wreaths at their centers. Each shop front is decorated in the same style, awnings of red laced with green garlands, golden lights and candy-cane ribbons adorning windows and doors.

We're wide-eyed and awestruck as Merry and Jolly pull us directly toward the gigantic Christmas tree at the top of the street decorated in much the same style. The star on top winks at us, beckoning us closer to the small crowd of elves waiting in welcome.

Before we're even out of the sleigh, a choir starts up with an a cappella medley of Christmas carols, and I automatically reach for Cole and Natalie's hands on either side of me.

Everything is beautiful, but it's also really intense after the calm and peaceful quiet of Puutyöt.

"Welcome to Pehmolelu, dear friends," a tiny female Christmas elf greets us cheerfully, and perhaps a bit shrilly, once the choir has finished.

At just over three feet tall, the friendly elf possesses an effervescent energy that makes her feel like a giant. Maybe a couple of giants. Her traditional knee-length elvish dress is bright red and green. Elaborate golden stitching stands out starkly on her sleeves, and a fluffy white collar covers her neck. Her pointed hat is bigger than her head, and the jingle bell on its tip is so large it puts the six on my horns to shame.

"Thank you for having us," Cole says politely. He gestures to the elves standing around the Christmas tree and to the choir. "This is such a warm reception. I'm Cole, this is Jasper, and that's Natalie."

The Christmas elf claps her hands and does a couple of tiny jumps before looking back at the other elves expectantly. They echo her clapping and add in whistles and cheers.

When they quiet down she rambles off her plans for us. "We're so excited to have you here. We've taken the liberty of organizing a schedule for you. First, we'll take you to put some warm food in your bellies, then you can go around and visit some of the shops. You know, do a little shopping, taste the local food. We make the best cookies in the North Pole and you just have to try them." In a conspiratorial whisper she adds, "Maybe you can boast about them to the other villages. If you like them, of course." Changing back to her default bright voice, she says, "Tomorrow is all about our workshop and you can each make your own teddies. It'll give you a great opportunity to see what we do and how it can help the children. Everyone needs a teddy."

I glance at Cole and scream at him with my eyes that this was not part of the plan. He smiles at me, then crouches down to talk to her. "That sounds wonderful. I'm sorry, I didn't catch your name."

"Oh, silly me." She giggles. "I'm Twinkle Tinselbottom. But you can just call me Twinkle."

I clear my throat and suppress my smile. Natalie and I do our best not to make eye contact.

Cole continues kindly, "It's nice to meet you, Twinkle. Is there somewhere we can maybe refresh before the tour starts?"

Thank fuck he asked that. The plug Natalie chose for me is a vibrating one. She and Cole took turns switching it on at random times throughout the journey, edging me all day. I really want to get them in a private room soon so we can take care of my very pressing needs. We weren't exactly planning on having such a jam-packed schedule as soon as we arrived.

"Of course. There's a bathroom in the restaurant we're going to. My mom is the best cook and has been working on her soup all day. She opened her shop in..." I tune the rest of the backstory out and tilt my head at my mates, needing them to do something before Twinkle moves us into the town permanently.

Natalie smirks at me and shakes her head, her eyes implying this is a consequence of my dare last night.

Cole listens patiently to Twinkle's story, clearly less affected by her high voice than I am. I'm not sure if he's indulging her in order to prolong my edging or if he's genuinely interested, but his tone is friendly when he says, "Wow, what a lovely story. I'm starving and look forward to the hearty meal your mother has prepared." That makes me frown at him because he knows exactly how needy I'm feeling, and now I'm sure he's just playing with me.

"So, Twinkle. Tell us more about the town. Are you the mayor?" Natalie asks. My mouth turns down at her also joining in on my torture, vowing to myself that I'm going to make her—both of them—pay for it when we're alone... eventually.

Twinkle giggles, folding in half like it's the funniest thing she's ever heard. "Mayor? I wish. But that is the best compliment I've ever received. I'm definitely writing it in my manifestation diary. I'm in charge of the welcoming committee."

My eyebrows shoot up, suddenly interested in that tidbit of information. "Oh, do you receive many guests?"

"Only Santa. He's really nice. But I started the committee when he told us you will be visiting. We even got you a bed big enough to fit all three of you together," Twinkle explains with such a broad smile I can see her molars.

Natalie chokes on a laugh. "That's very kind of you."

"My cousin Candy heard her aunt tell her mom that you had to sleep on the floor in Puutyöt. That is not okay. Our village will do better."

"It's not a competition, Twinkle. But we thank you for the forethought," Cole says calmly.

Twinkle narrows her eyes at him. "But if it was, we'd be winning. Right?"

Unable to hold back any longer, a laugh bursts out of me. "You're for sure winning with festivities and the best welcome ceremony we have received."

Twinkle looks over her shoulder as if to check if the other elves heard that proclamation. When she turns back to us, her cheeks are pink and her eyes filled with tears. "Thank you," she squeaks out and dabs at her cheeks. "Let's walk this way. Blinky and Glitzy will take care of your reindeer. They're my other cousins, so you can trust them. Santa does."

The meal ends up being just as delicious as she promised it would be. Twinkle is incredibly endearing once the jitters have worn off. She tells us many stories about the village, the type of toys they produce, and about all her career aspirations. After dinner, she leads us around the town square and we pop into a few shops, sampling all kinds of cookies until we're uncomfortably full.

Everyone is delightful and has a story ready for us, but this day is dragging on longer than even my sunny disposition can handle.

Sensing I'm nearing my limit, Cole excuses us for the rest of the night. "Thank you for everything. It's been a wonderful day, but I think it's best if we head to bed soon."

"Silly me," Twinkle says and taps her forehead. "You must be tired. Let me show you to your cottage."

Cole holds up both hands. "That's okay. Just point us in the right direction. I'm sure we can find it."

Twinkle rattles off the directions to our cottage. I don't even take in the festive decorations outside, just kick my shoes off at the door and fall face first onto the tartan-covered bed, my bells jingling with the force of my surrender.

"You tired?" Natalie purrs, lifting my sweater and running her hand up my back.

"Needy," I mumble against the blankets. "I've been hard all day. I need to cum or I might quite literally explode." I stick my lower lip out in a pout, turning my head so she can see and take pity on me.

"Does my puppy need some attention?"

"All the attention. Please," I say, not even minding her use of "puppy." I flip onto my back, starfishing the bed.

"Cole, it's time."

I whip my head around to find Cole and quirk my head at his expression. He's leaning against the doorjamb, a hint of nerves pulling at his mouth, but there's affection and excitement sparkling in his eyes.

Natalie pulls me into a sitting position and takes my hand. "We have a surprise for you. Cole, can you show him?"

Cole nods once and pads over to us. For the first time, I notice his walk is different than it usually is. Concern pulls my brows low and I'm about to ask him about it, but Natalie places her fingers on my forehead and smooths out my frown.

"Shhh, let him show you. Questions later."

Natalie stands behind Cole and undoes his belt with deft fingers. She lowers his pants, and like the good puppy I am, my mouth waters when Cole's cock springs free. I reach for it, but Natalie grabs my hand, redirecting it to Cole's ass. I lock eyes with him, a question in mine and assurance in his.

Reaching around, my fingers make contact with an object that has all the blood draining from my face, only to be funneled into my cock.

"Oh, you like that. Do you want to see?" Natalie asks. I can only nod in response, keeping my eyes locked with Cole's. Thankfully, she takes charge. I find myself overwhelmed by this moment, and by the look on Cole's face, I'd guess he's feeling quite the same.

She turns Cole and pulls his head to her shoulder so he's slightly bent over. I lower my face to his ass and pull his cheeks apart. There, nestled between two perfect buns is a plug the color of Natalie's eyes. I flick my gaze up at her and she smirks back at me, like she knows all the thoughts going rampant in my brain.

"Cole's been wearing this all day, same as us. I've been helping him for a while now to work up to bigger sizes," Natalie explains. I can only blink as I process her masterminding.

"Jas," Cole says, his voice raspy as he looks at me over his shoulder. "I want you to fuck me."

"I don't want to hurt you," I say, even as every instinct within me is begging me to bury my dick in his ass.

Cole turns around and cups my face. "As my fated mate,

I'm made to take you, just as Natalie is. Besides, you'll go slow our first time."

"First time?" I swallow. Hard. "You think there will be more?"

Cole's smile is cocky. "If the filthy plans Natalie and I have for us have anything to do with it, then definitely. We have our whole lives ahead of us. Of course there will be more."

I turn my head to kiss his wrist, then pull him down on my lap. "We're going to have to prep you really well."

"Let me," Natalie says and the gleam in her eyes tells me all I need to know. "But first, get naked. Now." Like two obedient puppets, we strip out of our clothes like the garments are on fire, dropping them in a pile on the floor. I sweep away the thousands of tiny pillows on the bed, and plop onto my back.

Cole crawls up over my legs and straddles my hips, my cock kissing his.

Natalie tears her sweater over her head. "You can touch each other, but no one gets to come until I say so. Jas, you can keep Cole nice and busy while I get him ready for you."

Cole leans down and whispers against my lips, "When did I get so compliant? And why do I like it so much?"

"When it's your fated mate giving you orders and she's really good at wringing maximum pleasure from your body."

"True, that'll do it," he says and kisses me, ravenously. Our tongues caress and dance, our hands grab and stroke, our cocks grinding against each other as my mate kisses me like I'm sunshine after a storm.

Cole pulls away with a gasp, a trembling whimper falling from him. "So… good…"

I peer around him to see a naked Natalie kneeling on the bed behind Cole, her puckered nipples begging to be toyed with. Her gaze is riveted on Cole's ass as she works the plug in and out, Cole rocking into her movements.

"That's a good boy, Coley," Natalie praises. "You're stretching so well for Jasper."

I want to watch his ass, watch him stretch for me, but right now, my mate needs my words.

"You're doing great, Cole. I can't wait to be inside you. I want to feel you wrapped around my cock. I'll make it so good for you." I run my hands over his shoulders, up his neck, and bring his face down to me so I can pepper him with kisses and more praise.

Cole pants, whimpers, squirms, pushing himself back onto Natalie's hand, and my heart squeezes at him being so willingly pliant. Having him give up control is a huge step and I don't take this shift in dynamics lightly.

"Oh, Cole, you have the most beautiful ass. Jasper and I are going to take such good care of you." Making eye contact with me, Natalie beckons me to her with a tilt of her head. "He's ready. Get over here, Jasper."

I place a final kiss to Cole's forehead and slip out from underneath him. Natalie moves over to give me some space and says to Cole, "Elbows and knees, Cole. We need to get the best angle."

Cole's whole body trembles with her command, his blush visible from this angle as he eagerly lowers himself onto his elbows.

"Where's the lube?" I ask Natalie, not seeing anywhere on the bed. The grin she gives me is pure devilry.

"I'm the lube." She smirks and grabs my hand, trailing my fingers through her wet pussy.

"Fuuuuck." Unable to resist, I push two fingers into her entrance, swirling them around to cover them in her slick. I keep my eyes on her as I coat my cock with her essence, repeating the process until my cock is glistening.

"Do you want to take his plug out?" Natalie asks a little breathlessly.

"You do it."

Natalie smiles and works the plug out gently, Cole gripping the blankets with the effort to remain still.

"Cole," I say reverently. "You look so good. Are you ready for me?"

Cole nods and pushes his ass back toward me. Natalie moves to the top of the bed and tilts his face up to look at her. "Words, Cole. Jasper needs your words."

"Can I...?"

"Anything you want or don't want, Cole. We stop right now if you're uncomfortable."

Cole straightens his arms and looks at Natalie and then at me. "I want us all to be connected for this. If that's okay?"

"Of course," Natalie says, instantly understanding him. "Where do you want me?"

"Underneath me, even if you're still topping both of us. I want to bury my cock in your pussy as Jasper fucks us."

Natalie gives him the sweetest smile full of so much love that it's almost like I can feel it burning in my chest.

She scoots down the bed and cradles his hips between her thighs. "Get that candy-cane cock in my cunt, Cole. Fill me up."

Cole enters her in a single thrust, but when he goes to draw back she digs her black-painted nails into his ass cheeks. "Tsk-tsk, Coley. You don't get to do that. Jasper's going to fuck us. You're going to let him move your body the way he wants. Going to let him fuck you deeper in to me. Got it?"

Cole nods, but at the reprimand in her arched brow, lets out a strained, "Yes."

I grip his ass and position my cock at his stretched

entrance. "Relax for me, Cole. We're going to start with just the tip."

Cole breathes out slowly as Natalie trails a hand up and down his back, her other hand cupping the back of his head. I push forward and let out a strained breath as my tip slides in easily.

The feeling of Natalie being here as Cole surrenders his body to me, after so many years, is almost more than I can bear. My heart floods with warmth and goose bumps dot my skin as my emotions war with my need to drive my cock forward.

"Fuck, Cole. You feel so good. You're doing so well. I'm going to give you a couple more inches, okay?"

Cole nods, but at Natalie's hands tightening on him, he pants, "Good. Give me more. Please."

I focus on my pacing, thrusting in slowly as Natalie whispers words of encouragement to us until I'm buried to the hilt. "So good, my loves. You're both doing so well."

Heavy breathing fills the room, words of love, promises, and vows as the three of us connect our bodies and souls.

It feels like the final hurdle being crossed as I start thrusting and we claim each other as mates with every piece of our hearts and souls.

24

Cole

We only stay in Pehmolelu for a couple of days before we go on to Pyörä. The news of our visits travels fast, and it feels like each village tries to top the previous one.

We all kind of miss the calm of Puutyöt, but we're still on a mission to find the perfect idea for the Naughty List.

The paddle we made in Puutyöt is purely for our own use and not a viable option as a gift for children. The teddies from Pehmolelu are cute keepsakes, three mini bear versions of us that will have a prime spot in our house, but they still don't feel like they will resonate with all children.

Pyörä was fun, but only because Natalie and Jasper taught me how to ride a bike. Living in the snow means I don't have much need for one, but when they heard I hadn't learned before, they made it their mission to teach me. I may have wobbled a couple of times and fallen once, maybe twice, but I figured it out in the end.

The drawing Natalie made of me on the bike will definitely get framed. She's mentioned buying some watercolors when we get back home—*our* home—to add to the nutcrackers, the cycling sketch, the sleigh, and the one of Jasper.

A strange calm settles over me as we near Kirja, the final village on our tour around the North Pole. I don't know if we'll find what we need to, but this entire adventure has been worth it. Not only has the bond between us strengthened, but the knowledge that we have the rest of our lives for... more, for... everything, has me looking forward to my future for the first time in ages. My heart fills with contentment and so much love for my mates, it feels like I'm glowing from the inside out.

"Um..." Natalie starts, and I turn my head slightly to give her my attention while also keeping my eyes trained on Merry and Jolly's backs. "Cole, did you maybe just have some cutesy feelings? Like, did you think of something nice?"

My brow creases. "How do you...? The bond!" I answer my own question.

Jasper leans forward and looks at us, eyes the size of saucers with unconstrained excitement. "You felt that too? I thought it was only me."

Natalie rubs at her chest with a gloved hand. "I've been feeling some emotions over the last couple of days, but I thought it was just all the warm and fuzzies you guys are giving me," she explains, pretty much reflecting my own thoughts.

"The bond must be strengthening!" Jasper exclaims. Merry lets out a grunt at the sudden noise, flicking his head in agitation. I mentally apologize to the reindeer, but I'm too elated at the news to be overly concerned with him right now.

"Don't go feeling bad for Merry. He's just jealous," Jasper teases.

"Fuck! Did you feel that too?" I ask, shocked how quickly he could pick that up.

"Now that I know where your emotions sit in my heart, it's easy to find you," Jasper explains. "Our bond is like a golden thread connecting us, your emotions bright at the other end." Turning to Natalie, he continues, "And our bond is cherry red, just like your lips. Can you feel this?"

A breath shudders out of me and my blood goes straight to my cock with the emotions Jasper pumps down the bond, and I almost get images, but that can't be right.

Natalie shifts in her seat like she got the exact same thing I did. "Are you sending us visuals too?" Her voice sounds just as breathy as mine feels, would I be able to talk now.

"Fuck! This is exciting! Oh, the games we can play sending suggestions to each other at inappropriate times," Jasper babbles, dancing in his seat and making the sleigh swerve with the movement.

"You mean like this?" I can feel Natalie's concentration as she pushes an image through our bond, and I have to blink hard to keep my focus on the road. It does the job of shutting Jasper up, though. I glance at him staring at her open-mouthed, his eyes calculating, most probably trying to think if it's possible.

"Jasper." There's no real censure in my tone, but I need to put an end to their line of thinking before he convinces Natalie to actually try to straddle his face right here in the sleigh. That just sounds like an accident waiting to happen.

Thankfully, the first buildings of Kirja come into view at that time and we all fall quiet as we approach the village.

The snow here is the palest pink and covers less than what we've seen in other villages. It dusts the sloped roofs in a thin layer, and powders the low stone walls lining the narrow road. It's almost like I have the desire to stop the sleigh and dig my hands into the snow, to breathe some kind of life into it to make it fluffy and bright like it's meant to be.

Round windows filled with warm light, smoking chimneys made of stone, and doors with plain wreaths of pine make the houses feel like they're more suited for a fairytale than here.

Lanterns dotted along the stone wall light up in turn as we near them, leading us into the center of town. There are no elaborate garlands or choirs waiting to greet us, but the village's quaint charm speaks louder than the brightest decorations.

Cole and Natalie must feel it too, because Natalie silently places a hand on my thigh and reaches for Jasper's hand with her other as our sleigh whooshes down the street.

Piercing the peaceful quiet, the reindeer's grunts signal our arrival as we pull up to the guest cottage. The front door creaks open and an ancient elf steps out. A bushy mustache perches on his top lip, the corners twirled in a perfect handlebar. His pointed ears droop with age and delicate half-moon glasses balance on the tip of his nose.

As one, we get out of the sleigh and stand a few steps down from the four-foot-tall elf.

"Welcome to Kirja," he says, his voice low and rich. "I'm Quill Evergreen. You three are a sight for my sore old eyes."

There's something instantly likable about him. Like I want to sit with him for hours and hear his stories from back in the day.

I hold a hand out, ready to shake his gently. "I'm Cole. These are my mates, Natalie and Jasper."

"Hi, Quill," Natalie says, giving him a small wave as he places a warm hand in mine.

"Now that's a story I would love to hear." The smile that follows transforms Quill's face. It's like the thought of a good story melts the years off him, his hooded eyes twinkling with a new light.

"I volunteer as storyteller," Jasper says, raising his hand. "And Natalie has drawings to match. Though, she might have to be selective of which ones to show you," he adds with a wink.

A full belly laugh rumbles out of Quill, his shoulders shaking with mirth. "I can only imagine. Let's get you inside. It hasn't snowed in ages, but you never know, tonight might be the night."

"You guys go in. I'll join you once I get the reindeer settled in the stables." I head back to Merry and Jolly, giving them lots of pets and praise for their good work. I unhook their harnesses from the sleigh and grab their bridles, leading them toward the back of the cottage where the reindeer stables usually are.

Thanks to us accepting our fated bond, we no longer have the distance restriction in place. If one of us wants to go somewhere alone, we are now free to do so. However, stepping away from my mates to settle the reindeer is as far as I want to go.

After I get them tucked in, I take a moment to look up at the clear sky, finding the North Star directly above me. Breathing in deeply, I search for my mate bonds and find Jasper's and Natalie's without much effort. Their humor and joy courses through me as traces of their laughter float from the house.

The focus on them must be why I don't hear someone approaching.

"Um, hi, Cole."

I turn around abruptly, gasping as my heart pounds wildly at the sight before me. "Father?"

"I'm sorry. I didn't mean to startle you."

My father looks years older than the last time I saw him. His hair is all white, and the full beard he used to be proud of is shorter than I've ever seen it, only a little longer than stubble. Melancholy seeps from him, and something uncomfortable twists in my chest.

"Are you okay?" I ask him, really concerned for his well-being now that my heart rate is stabilizing.

Ignoring the question, he says, "You look well. Happy." For the first time, a hint of a smile pulls at his mouth, and the light twinkle that all Santas have threatens to make an appearance in his eyes.

"I'm mated. I'm very happy," I state honestly, my satisfied grin impossible to keep off my face.

"Congratulations. That's wonderful." My father looks like he really means that too. His hands flex at his sides like he wants to reach out and pat my shoulder or something.

"Thank you." I'm grateful for his kind words, but unsure about why I'm having this conversation outside the stables right now. "What are you doing here? Do you live in Kirja?" I ask, needing some kind of indication of why he orchestrated this meeting.

My father swallows hard, his Adam's bobbing with the movement. "Close by. I heard you were heading this way and I wanted to take the opportunity to talk to you. To apologize."

I tilt my head, confused by this whole interaction. "To apologize for what?" My tone is curious, all the hurt from when I was young replaced by worry for him.

"Everything. I—"

"Cole! Where are you?" Jasper calls from the cottage.

"Cole! Are you okay?" Natalie's voice follows, a flicker of anxiety spiking our bond.

Jasper comes barreling around the corner, Natalie following close behind, squinting her eyes to find us.

Heaving in heavy breaths, Jasper pats my body down, muttering, "You're okay. You're okay." I grip his hands to comfort him. My shock at seeing my father must've echoed through the bond.

Natalie comes to a stop in front of me, her back to mine,

as she stares down my father with her hands fisted in her hips.

"What do you want with him?" she hisses, puffing out her chest like she's readying for a fight.

"Hi, Natalie," my father says calmly. "I'm glad you still have all that spunk you had as a kid." The shock that courses through Natalie has me laying a steadying hand on her shoulder. Jasper joins her other side, lacing their fingers together.

"What the fuck?" she asks, most likely thrown by him mentioning her childhood. Santas have great memories, and judging by that line, my father remembers her well.

A pleased expression pulls my father's lips into a smile that resembles mine, and for the first time, I can see parts of me in him. I wonder if we have any other similarities that I've missed.

"I don't think you'd remember me, but we met once when you were supposed to be sleeping and I placed a certain princess-themed coloring book under your tree. You must have been about five years old at the time," he says fondly.

Natalie gasps and takes a step back into my chest. "That was real?" she whispers.

"I'm afraid so." He winks at her before shifting his kind gaze to Jasper. "Hi, Jasper. Nice to see you again. How are your parents?" With every sentence out of his mouth, he becomes more alive, his expressions warming up as he relaxes around us.

Jasper bows his head slightly, his bells jingling with the movement. "It's good to see you too, sir. My parents are great. Loved up and living in the Alps, still."

"Good." He clasps his hand together, wringing them slightly as nerves return. "I'm sorry to barge in on your visit. I heard you were coming and I couldn't resist seeing Cole again. It's been so long. Too long."

I swallow, feeling sad for a male who has clearly been hurting for a long time. "Have you had dinner?" I ask.

My father shakes his head. "Don't worry about me. You kids have fun." He cups his hand around his mouth like he wants to tell us a secret, whispering, "And don't tell anyone, but Kirja is my favorite village."

"None of us have eaten yet. Join us." My invitation comes out as a demand, but I need to know why he came to find me. Why now?

"Damn it, Nick. Don't make this more awkward. The children are hungry and so are you," Quill calls from somewhere behind me. It's so weird to hear someone call my father Nick, but it seems to do the trick.

My father huffs a laugh that sounds so much like mine that Natalie and Jasper both turn to give me a curious look. I give them a one-shouldered shrug, because I don't know what else to say.

My father nods. "All right. Dinner sounds lovely."

25

Natalie

inner is awkward as fuck.

The sound of forks scraping against plates as we sit around the—thankfully large—table makes my eye twitch. Despite how delicious Quill's chicken pot pie is, the atmosphere is making it hard to really enjoy the effort the old elf put into the dish. Now that I have a clear read on my mates' emotions, thanks to the bond, I am constantly aware of their discomfort on top of my own.

After some strained polite conversation about the weather—newsbreak, it's snowy and cold—Jasper clears his throat and puts on his sunny mask. "So, Quill, tell us more about Kirja. What kind of books do you typically send out at Christmas?"

Quill sits back and twirls the end of his impressive mustache. "I've been in charge of production for many, many years—perhaps too many years—but it's never been as slow as it's been lately. Children want fancy toys nowadays and the request for books for Christmas is down."

"I love books," Jasper says excitedly. "I wish I can get a

book, or twenty, for Christmas. Take note, mates," he adds with a wink.

An amused smile lifts Quill's mouth. "If only more children would wish for that, then the village would be thriving again."

Concern draws Cole's brows down. "Is it affecting the village too?"

"Oh yes," Quill nods sadly. "Many have relocated to Joulu or moved to neighboring villages. It seems that the fondness for books they once had, is not quite what it used to be. They've gone on to explore other passions, other crafts."

"Doesn't that leave you in an even more difficult situation with less workers available?" Cole asks, quick to see the business angle.

Quill sighs, his mustache vibrating with the strength of his breath. "In a way, it does. But, we make do."

We lapse into silence again, but something that's been tickling at the back of my mind stirs as an idea starts to take shape. First though, I need to redirect the conversation back to Cole's father and his reason for being here.

My innate desire to call Daddy Santa out on his shit and to fix things for my mate rides me hard. Deciding we've pussyfooted enough, I put down my knife and fork and look at all the males around the table.

"Okay, boys. This is about as much awkwardness as I can handle. So, let's have some real talk."

They blink back at me, and Cole places his hand on my thigh. Once, my default setting would've made me believe it's an act to stop me from speaking, but I smile to myself as Cole's admiration and thankfulness floods the bond. On my other side, Jasper mirrors the move, his bond lighting up with amusement.

Leaning over, Jasper whispers against my ear, "I like it

when you get all bossy." He squeezes my thigh and sits back up before I can respond to that delicious innuendo.

Across the table, Nick Senior nods at me and I swear that's approval flashing in his eyes. "Cole and Jasper are very lucky to have you." Try as I might, I can't help but preen a little under that compliment, especially when he's delivered it with such sincerity.

I tilt my head in thanks. "Feeling's mutual about them. Maybe now is a good time to tell us why you're here? And why you approached Cole after so many years of not seeing him?"

He runs a hand over his short beard and his mouth turns up a fraction. "I do want to tell you all of that. For a minute, I had hoped to have a private conversation with Cole, but he deserves to hear my apology in front of his mates too."

Quill raises his brows. "I can go if you'd like to keep this family only? But I'd be sad to miss what promises to be an interesting conversation." I appreciate Quill's candor. He kind of reminds me of an older Jasper, minus the horns and sex appeal.

Nick Senior shakes his head. "Please stay, Quill. As my oldest friend, you're part of my family."

I try not to find that endearing, but something tells me Nick Senior isn't the villain I've made him out to be in my head. I'm not going to go easy on him, though. Cole deserves to have someone fighting for him, and that someone is most definitely me.

Looking Cole squarely in the eyes, Nick Senior places a hand over his heart, his eyes shining with earnestness, as he says, "First of all, I want to apologize for putting you in charge of a job you dislike so much. Both you and Jasper. I thought by giving you the Naughty List, when Nick is in charge of the Nice List, would make you feel more part of the family and you two could grow close as brothers. I am deeply sorry about the way it has turned out. I had good intentions, but my execution was poor."

Oh, shit. His way of thinking kind of makes sense.

Cole's hand tightens imperceptibly on my thigh. "Thank you. I didn't exactly see things from that point of view before."

Nick Senior reaches toward Cole before putting his hand back on his heart. "And that's my fault for not explaining properly. When Cole was born, I felt so guilty because I broke from tradition by having another child. It wasn't fair to Cole, nor to Nick, nor to Cole's mother, or my late wife's memory. I've let grief and my guilt keep me isolated, thinking everyone is better off without me interfering in their lives. Recently, I have started realizing the errors of my ways and would like to make amends. If you'd let me, of course."

Holy fuck. This guy knows how to do apologies.

No stopping him now, the apology train hits my other mate next. "Jasper, I apologize for pulling you into this too. Just because things have always been done a certain way, doesn't mean we have to continue doing them so. Your parents enjoyed their job back in the day, but things don't have to continue like that."

I know I haven't known my mates for long, but my soul sighs in relief at the closure between them and Nick Senior, so I can only imagine how monumental it is for them… Cole, especially. I lace my fingers with my mates', lending them all the silent support I can as they process all of these revelations.

"Thank you, sir. That means a lot," Jasper croaks. Clearing his throat, he asks, "So you're good with us finding different ways to change the Naughty List?"

Nick Senior nods emphatically. "Of course. I only wish I had thought of it myself first. I have never challenged traditions. I just did what my father did, and his father before him." He swallows hard and his voice breaks as he continues, "But seeing you take on this mission, this quest, to find something better, to help children, to inspire them, it's been eye-opening. And if you were so inclined, I'd like to have another chance at maybe getting to know each other."

Cole's breath hitches. "You've been following our mission?"

"Oh yes. Nick messaged me when you left. Asked me why I didn't help you sooner, and I've been kicking myself since. I've also been checking in with Quill as updates filter in from the other villages. My cabin is here, on the edge of Kirja, and I've been readying myself for you and your mates' arrival. I may have practiced my apology a couple hundred times, but above all else, I just desired to see you again, and to maybe have the honor of meeting your mates—the newest members of our family."

Now feeling calmer after getting a read on Nick Senior's intentions, I replace my antagonistic tone with genuine curiosity. "So, while we're on the topic of family and wanting Cole to be part of it… Why name him Cole when that's literally what the naughty kids get?"

Nick Senior winces. "Ah, firstly, this is a poor excuse, but I'll try my best to explain it. The connection between Cole—C-O-L-E—and coal—C-O-A-L—didn't enter my mind at the time of naming him. You see, the names 'Cole' and 'Nick' both mean the exact same thing. Maybe I've never stated it clearly, but it's a beautiful meaning that I also have the privilege of sharing. It means 'victory of the people.' I always meant for Cole and Nick to be a team—a unit, if you will—working together toward making Christmas special for people all around the world."

Cole tilts his head to the side, astonishment lacing his tone as he asks, "Cole and Nick have the same meaning?"

A glum smile twists Nick Senior's lips. "They do."

Quill slaps his friend's shoulder. "Nick, why haven't you ever told him this? I remember how excited you were when he was born. Scared too, yes. But you were so excited to have the perfect name."

A defeated sigh drifts from Nick Senior. "I was a fool. Still am in many ways. Though, I'll be trying my utmost for a second chance to be part of Cole and his mates' lives. If they'll allow me."

"Not gonna lie, that's kind of cute," Jasper says. The tension breaks as we laugh at his remark.

Feeling Cole's emotions throughout this conversation flow from apprehension to empathy and finally blooming with hope, has me feeling very optimistic about his relationship with his father.

When the laughter tapers off, I fake a sulk that would make Jasper proud. "Ugh, sucks to say, but this is all kind of redeeming Nick Senior in my eyes."

Nick Senior reaches across the table and I give him my hand. His is warm and calloused, speaking to his many years of toy making. The last threads of my apprehension melt away when he focuses his sincerity on me. "That means a lot to me. I am not taking your tentative approval lightly. I hope that over the years we can all get to know each other and I can make up for all the wrong that I've done."

Jasper clutches his heart dramatically. "You've got to stop with the sweet sayings. My heart is going to burst with all these gooey feelings."

I let go of Nick Senior's hand and straighten my shoulders. "While we're on the topic of gooey feelings," I start hesitantly, "I think I have an idea for the Naughty List."

Quill brings his hands together in an exuberant clap. "Oh, how marvelous. You four go chat in the living room and I'll bring you some eggnog," he offers and starts to gather our empty plates.

"I'm hoping to hear your opinion on this too, Quill," I say.

Quill pauses and looks at me over his half-moon glasses. "Me?"

"I hope so."

"Okay. Can't wait to hear what it is. But I still need my eggnog. In my old age, I can't sleep well without it."

"Let me help you," Nick Senior offers. He stands up to take the plates from his friend and for a minute, I almost forgot how tall Santas are. Despite Quill being quite literally half his size, they seem to have an ease about them that comes from years of companionship.

Jasper, Cole, and I head for the antique two-seater couch covered in a rich crimson velvet. Like it's second nature by now, Jasper pulls me onto his lap and Cole puts my legs across his thighs, gently massaging my sock-clad feet.

"Thank you for speaking up for me," Cole says, his eyes misting with gratefulness. "If you hadn't come into our lives, I would've still been walking around with so much hurt based on misunderstandings. In such a short time, you've torn walls down and sped up timelines. You're the reason we're healing and thriving. If I didn't believe the fates had sent you before, I am a big fucking believer now. Thank you." Cole's final words come out on a choked whisper, the corners of his mouth pulled down with gratitude.

I take his hand in mine and press a kiss to his knuckles. "I'll always fight for our happiness, no matter how many lines I have to cross. Fixing things between you and Daddy Santa is all part of that. I'm only happy when my mates are happy."

Jasper wraps his arms around my waist and pulls me closer. "Our lives have literally changed because of you. We are so thankful for every single thing you've said and done, and what you're apparently still doing. Why didn't you tell us about your idea sooner?" I detect a hint of hurt in Jasper's voice as he buries his nose in my hair.

I lean back and cup his face so I can meet his eyes. "It's something that's slowly been brewing in my mind over the last few days. But after hearing more tonight, I think it might work. I wanted to be sure before I said anything."

Cole cups my ankle, his thumb tracing gentle patterns across my leggings. "Whatever it is, we're in."

"Just because we're mated, doesn't mean you have to blindly follow everything I say."

Cole chuckles. "We know. But we also know *you* and how your brilliant mind works. Based on overwhelming evidence, we can already deduce that it's going to be an ingenious plan." I push my love and appreciation down the bond to both my mates just as the two other males enter the room.

"Okay, Natalie," Nick Senior says after a sip of his well-spiced eggnog. "How can we be of assistance with your plan?"

"It's actually quite straightforward. Jasper writes children's stories. I draw. Cole loves books and does binding as a hobby. Quill is tired and this village needs a makeover. And you, Daddy Santa, have the knowledge to know if a good children's book will work as a replacement for coal for Christmas. Would our book inspire kids to enact enough change in their lives… to get on the Good List?"

"That's clever," Nick Senior says, ignoring my Daddy Santa moniker. "I think for this to work, it would need to be a really good story. One with a clear message. Something that would captivate them and make them look forward to next Christmas."

I look around the room to see their reactions, each male carefully considering my proposal before giving me feedback. I appreciate them taking the time and not just humoring me with positive responses.

Jasper is the first to break out of his thinking trance. "How the Children Helped the Nutcrackers Save Christmas," he says slowly, his smile growing bigger and more confident with each word.

I nod back at him. "That was the story that first had me thinking of the idea."

Quill drops his chin and looks at us over the rim of his glasses. "You already have a story?"

Cole sits up a little straighter, his eyes sparkling. "It's perfect. Jasper's story is practically ready to go. We can use many of the drawings from Natalie's sketchbook as illustrations. If we formatted the story well, this could really be inspirational."

"Natalie, can you show us your drawings?" Nick Senior asks, putting down his glass as his own excitement grows.

Underneath me, Jasper is practically squirming in his seat, his legs bouncing as the whole room's energy shifts with the idea of finally finding something that could work.

"Jasper, get your story ready. I'll transcribe," Quill offers, downing the last dregs of his eggnog.

We spend the rest of the night ironing out details and fine-tuning the story. I make notes of new drawings I'll add, and which ones I've completed that we'll use. Cole chats to Quill about what kind of paper would work best and which materials they'll use for the cover, and how many extra workers they'll need to complete the book in time for Christmas.

By the time morning comes, we're exhausted and exhilarated. We video call Nick with our plan, the complete story, and rough sketches in hand.

And, we get his approval.

I think we may have just saved Christmas for every child on the Naughty List.

26

Jasper

"Jas, you look snazzy," Natalie says brightly, inspecting the silver tinsel she just zigzagged between my horns. I do a spin for her and pretend the living room is my personal catwalk, strutting my way across it to show off my new festive look.

Now that we've been in Kirja for the last couple of months, I've stopped wearing bells on my horns—there's only so much jingling I could handle. Instead, Natalie has taken it upon herself to find an array of accessories to decorate them with. Since tinsel seems to be in abundant supply today, thanks to it being our official Christmas Decorating Day, I'm not surprised that some has found its way onto my horns.

"Why, thank you, my dear," I say and squeeze her delectable ass. "Later, I want you spread out under this tree, wearing nothing but tinsel." I can already imagine how much fun it would be unwrapping her like she's our favorite present.

"That can be arranged." Natalie winks at me before sauntering over to Cole with his own string of silver tinsel. She arranges it in a sparkly scarf around his neck and my heart shimmers at the sight. They look beautiful together—relaxed and cozy, and… *mine.*

This year, Christmas approached way faster than expected. Since the moment Nick approved our pitch for our Nutcracker tale, we've been running full steam ahead to get the story and illustrations ready, and the right quantities produced. No coal needed this year.

It's amazing doing this with my mates. Each of us is involved in different parts of the book's creation, and working together as a team is so rewarding. Sharing ideas with them and planning for future Christmases, is more than I could have ever dreamed of.

We have even planned out more books, and not just for the Naughty List. Some of the stories I wrote in the Alps—stories I thought no one would ever read—have also been chosen by Nick Senior, Nick, and Quill to be published for *all* children. Natalie has already sketched out ideas for their illustrations so they can be ready for Christmas next year.

Because all three of us enjoy being hands-on, we have remained in Kirja. Quill has handed over the reins to Cole, remaining on long enough to oversee the transition before he can finally enjoy retirement. I think Nick Senior mentioned something about a long-overdue ice-fishing trip the two of them have planned.

I climb back onto the ladder next to our very own Christmas tree, a box of ornaments balanced precariously on the top rung.

"Can you turn on some music, please?" I ask Cole, wanting all the happy Christmas vibes this year, including obnoxious Christmas carols I can belt out at the top of my voice.

"Good idea. Twinkle sent me a link to an album the Pehmolelu choir recorded, and I haven't had a chance to listen to it yet," Cole says, flinging his tinsel scarf over his shoulder before reaching for his phone.

When the first notes of "Carol of the Bells" hits, I wiggle my butt like I'm right there in Pehmolelu, performing with them.

The last couple of months have been busy with renovations on the guest cottage to turn it into our permanent home. And now, it's finally time to decorate for our first Christmas together.

"This is looking gorgeous," Natalie says, handing me a couple of snowflake ornaments. "I know none of us have had spectacular Christmases so far, but this is shaping up to look like the best one ever."

"I'm pretty sure nothing can beat this. Ever. Having you…" My words break off as an unwelcome sensation roils through my body. I step down the ladder, bracing one hand against it as my jaws start to ache.

"Fuck," I say on a guttural groan.

"Jas, are you okay?" Cole asks, hands running all over my body, looking to find what's wrong.

"What's today's date?" I ask, bracing myself against the discomfort burning through my body, as well as the answer.

"December first," Natalie says carefully, running a comforting hand up and down my back.

I step back abruptly, frantically searching for an exit. "NO! No, no, no, no, no. I forgot. Oh, fuck. I forgot. No."

"Jas, what's wrong?" Natalie asks, reaching for my hand. I curl my fingers away, not wanting her to see my claws forming.

Cole connects the dots quickly. "How can we help you?"

"My krampus curse. It starts today. I need to leave." With each second that passes, I can feel my body transitioning, my legs slowly getting longer, hairier. My teeth sharpen and my voice deepens. I take another step toward the door. "I've got to go. I've got to go."

Natalie grabs my face between her hands and directs my gaze down to meet hers. "You're not going anywhere. We love you. In all your forms."

I shake my head. "But… but…"

She squeezes my face tighter between her hands, determination burning in her eyes. "No buts. No arguing. Now, what do you need from us?"

I try to shake my head again, but her hold is firm. "Nothing," I say, my voice low and gravelly as my beast takes over. "I need to go outside. I need to run."

Natalie quirks an eyebrow at me. "Do you want to chase me?"

My eyes widen and my cock grows hard at the thought of tracking Natalie through the forest out back, of sneaking up on her and tackling her down in the snow, and taking her roughly in this form. But I step back and quickly shake my head, trying to clear the image.

Cole places a gentle hand on my chest. "Jasper, don't try to fight your nature. We love all of you. Besides, we can feel how much you like that idea. If Natalie's offering, don't try to dissuade her. Our woman knows what she wants."

"It wouldn't be fair," I try to argue, even as my basest instincts scream at me to say yes. "I'm fast in this form. Stronger. Scary."

Natalie cups my cock straining in my suddenly very tight pants. "This is definitely not scary. It's enticing. And don't you remember I said I want to be chased?"

Before another protest can leave my mouth, Cole silences me with a look and takes my hand. "Come here," he says gently and takes Natalie's hand too, leading us to the back door. "I want to show you two something. I've been practicing a lot and was waiting until the perfect moment, but this might be the right time to reveal what I've been working on."

Natalie and Cole grab their coats and put on their boots. I proceed as is, since I have no need for shoes in this form, nor do they fit my much larger shape. We take the few steps down into the snow-covered backyard, and I breathe in deeply, savoring how heightened my senses are in this form. The scent of Natalie's arousal permeates the air as she looks her fill of my fully transformed body. Cole's lust blooms when he comes to a stand a few steps away from us, but his scent is tinged with a hint of excited nerves about what he wants to show us.

Behind Cole, the cloudless sky is a bruised blue and purple, signaling the approaching sunset and the first night of my weeklong curse.

Raising his hand in front of him, a soft smile tips Cole's lips up as tiny snowflakes appear out of nowhere and land in his palm. Delicate, pink, fluffy snowflakes.

My mouth falls open at the sight and Cole's grin stretches into pure bliss.

"How?" Natalie's question is a reverent whisper as her eyes take in the sight of our mate's snow magic.

"Watch this," Cole says, his excitement growing with our stunned awe of his new skills. He swirls his hands, forming three substantial spherical balls, and stacking them on top of each other to create the most charming snowman.

"Okay, Elsa, that deserves a hug," Natalie says after a moment of just taking it all in, and runs into Cole's arms.

I walk around the snowman, running a claw-tipped finger over the pink perfect spheres. "This is amazing, Cole. It's beautiful."

He tucks Natalie into his side and waves his fingers so a little flurry drifts down to cover their footprints. "My Santa magic activated when our mate bond snapped into place. I didn't know what it was at first, I just had this deep-seated desire to play with the snow. To connect with it, for lack of a better word. I've been experimenting for some time now and have a firm grasp on my ability. Nick was really excited when I told him."

"I'm so happy you've connected with both sides of your heritage," I say. "Nick and you can probably have a snow-off. Get it? Show-off, snow-off?"

Natalie snorts and Cole chuckles. "Thanks, Jas. In much the same way, Natalie and I want to connect with all parts of *you*, too. Including this full krampus mode."

There has been a whirlwind of changes since Natalie came into our lives. She's the spark that Cole and I needed to really start living. It's like we're finally recognizing all that we can be.

And it's time for me to take Natalie at her word too, to seize this opportunity to be my most basest self.

"Do you need a safe word?" I growl, giving over the beast rippling underneath my humanity.

Natalie smirks, delight flaming through our bond. "Nope. You can monitor my emotions."

Cole gives Natalie a firm kiss and swats her on the ass, lightly pushing her in the direction of the snow-covered forest behind the house. "Let's give Natalie a head start. I'll cover her tracks and stay behind to make sure no one approaches anywhere close to our house. You two have fun. I'll have blankets and hot drinks waiting for you when you get back. Tomorrow night I'll have my turn."

I grunt my agreement to his plan, but my feral gaze stays fixed on Natalie trembling with excitement.

"Run."

27

Natalie

Snow crunches underneath my feet as I sprint into the darkening forest. My heart pounds in my chest, echoing the thudding of my boots, and thrill courses through my veins as I finally get to live out a fantasy I've had for many years.

Somewhere behind me, the low rumbling of Jasper's beastly voice twines with Cole's calm tone. Thankfully I got a bit of a head start, but Jasper looks like he's fast in this form.

Yes, I want him to catch me, but I'm going to try my best to not make it too easy on him.

I zigzag between trees, double back, making sure Cole is still sending enough snow to cover my tracks, before sprinting off in a new direction again. The snow isn't too thick here, so it's still easy to spot fallen branches and to clamber over them without fear of twisting an ankle.

Over the last few months, Jasper mentioned that he has heightened senses in his full krampus mode—his hearing, sight, and scent are all improved, along with strength and speed. I suck in a breath and my pussy gets wet just thinking how I'll be at his complete mercy when he's so much bigger.

In his usual half-shifted form, he's tall enough that I fit right under his chin. But earlier outside the house, I had to crane my neck to look into his eyes. He's now probably around seven feet of lean muscle—then add in horns, a tail, an impressively long tongue, and his beautiful, thick cock.

A shiver runs through me, giving me another idea on how to trick him. I strip off my coat, and tie it to a fallen branch, dotting my scent on every other tree before bunching it up and hiding it in some shrubs. It might divert him for a little while, but I know I can't fool him forever.

I take off again, going as fast as my legs can carry me in the increasingly thicker snow, to put as much distance between Jasper and myself before he starts the chase.

Suddenly, a beastly growl tears through the forest and my adrenaline reignites, sending my feet forward even faster.

The forest stills. The whole atmosphere shifts as if even the trees are aware that a monster is on the hunt.

Low-hanging branches grab at my sweater, ripping off strips of wool, slowing my desperate speed. But I keep going, running as fast as my burning lungs will allow.

I jump over a rock, and pause. Leaning against a tree, I hold my breath, straining my ears for any sound that will indicate how far away Jasper is. My pulse drums so loudly that for a minute, it's all I can hear, drowning out any other indication of life in the forest.

Until it isn't.

A rumbling purr echoes through the quiet night. The gritting of snow under large, steady footsteps meticulously circling something sends anticipatory goose bumps skittering across my skin.

I try to take shallow breaths, bracing myself, as I realize Jasper is most likely stalking my coat.

"AAAAH!"

At the sound of Jasper's outraged cry, I take off again.

Running, running, running. I don't look back. Breaths saw in and out of my lungs, clouding the air, as I pump my arms, willing my legs to go faster.

A phantom wind blows against the back of my neck and I chance a glance backward.

I shouldn't have.

Long arms wrap around my body, sending me careening forward, but Jasper twists us around so he takes the brunt of the fall on his back. I try to scramble up, to crawl away, but Jasper is strong, fast.

He hooks long fingers around my ankle and pulls me back, flattening me against the snow with his naked body.

"Got you, little mate," Jasper growls into my ear, the timbre of his voice rumbling through the forest.

The sensation of his furry legs, his clawed fingers, and his monstrously big form against my back has me dripping for him, my pussy producing so much slick that it'll be ready to take Jasper's cock with ease.

His hands roam over me, tearing at my clothes with sharp claws, slicing through my leggings and underwear easily as he grinds his hard cock against my bare ass.

"Yes," I say, pushing back against him.

The cool kiss of the Arctic air is welcome against my heated skin, sobering me enough to check in on our bond. Jasper's need for me is front and center, burning with an intensity I've never felt, though there is a hint of concern for my safety and well-being. I push back with all my love and desire for him, giving him the green light on whatever he wants to do.

It's like pulling the pin on a grenade.

In a single move, Jasper lifts me onto my knees, maneuvering my body like I'm a rag doll made especially for him. He bundles my leggings and places them on the snow as a cushion, protecting my face from the cold, before pushing my upper body down and angling me exactly how he wants me.

"Now my mate will take my big fucking krampus cock," Jasper growls, and I feel the words reverberate through the very essence of my being.

He lifts my hips until my slick cunt is hovering above his cock, and he thrusts himself balls deep in a single move.

The sensation of being filled so quickly, so fully, when my adrenaline is still pumping through my veins, exceeds any expectations I had for our chase.

My bond with Cole brightens with his delight. He's clearly monitoring us from a distance, and I have enough presence of mind to send back a cheeky wink, knowing he'll be on the receiving end of this magnificent—and even larger —cock tomorrow.

Jasper holds my hips steady, fucking me hard and fast until my arms lose the strength to keep myself up. He shifts, lifting me into his lap, and bounces me up and down on his thick cock.

Our pleasure only increases as Cole sends images down the bond of him stroking himself along with us, climbing to completion together, until I fall over the edge and into oblivion with him.

Jasper fucks me through my release, until my throat is raw from moaning their names, wringing orgasm after orgasm from me.

"I need to bite you," Jasper rasps. "Knot you."

"Do it."

"It's gonna hurt."

"Jasper, do it."

Jasper nudges his knot inside my greedy cunt and bites down where my neck meets my shoulder. I scream as his teeth pierce the skin, but the pain soon morphs into pleasure as another orgasm rolls through me. He holds me tightly as his thrusts stutter, and he fills me up with his sweet cum.

After a couple of minutes where we catch our breath, Jasper scoops me into strong arms, knot still firmly locked inside me, and carries me home like some kind of cock Popsicle. I'm probably leaving a trail of our joint releases across the forest floor, but it's not possible to care any less about that when I'm happy and safe in my monster's arms.

"That was amazing."

"Are you talking to me?" I ask, not sure where exactly that came from.

Jasper stops walking, and his brows furrow. "You heard that?"

I think back on what he said about his parents, and attempt to send him a mental, *"Yes."*

Jasper's eyes widen, gleaming with excitement. *"I think the bite sealed our bond. We can now have telepathic conversations,"* he says into my mind.

"I can't wait for you to bite Cole tomorrow night. He's going to love it."

"I'm starting to see the wonderful benefits of being a krampus. On the fifth, when I'm at my most feral, I'm taking you both, together. And now I don't have to worry, because we can communicate even more clearly."

"Sign me up. But first, I need a bath and a nap."

"Anything you want, princess."

I shudder with contentment and tighten my hold around Jasper's shoulders, loving the way that nickname sounded.

The sight of Cole waiting for us in the living room, silhouetted by Christmas lights and holding blankets and drinks, has those pesky heart flutters starting up again. Flutters I'll never get tired of, because these males are everything to me.

I'm really looking forward to this coming week and the rest of our lives together.

Natalie: What's everyone doing for Christmas? Fancy a trip to the North Pole to join us?

Iris: Thank you for the generous offer, but Helena and I usually spend Christmases together somewhere warm. Dragging the males back to the Caribbean with us this time.

Natalie: That sounds fun! Feel free to visit anytime you want. It's an open invitation!

Sadie: A snowy Christmas sounds fantastic! We're in!

Natalie: Did I mention the snow here is pink?

Sadie: Girllll, my bags are already packed *sparkling heart emoji*

Florence: Let me ask Adelbert, but I'm sure he'll enjoy visiting the forest up north.

Natalie: Yay!

Diana: Will need to ask my males, but I'm sure I can convince them.

Natalie: *MY*? Yes, girl! Get it! Boss babe!

Sylvia: We'd love to maybe come next year, but Alice and Louisa are joining us in Paris for Christmas.

Cordelia: Me too! We're heading to South Africa for summer surfing and catching up with family, but would love to come next Christmas!

Natalie: Will miss you guys, but have fun and see you next year!

28

Cole

The streets of Kirja look completely different on Christmas morning than they did when we first arrived. Each house is decorated in its own unique style, loosely based on the family's favorite book.

Some streets have gone so far as to coordinate according to favorite authors or books in a series, stringing matching garlands between participating homes. It has been incredibly heartwarming to watch this community blossom over the past few months.

With the influx of fresh stories being written, families have returned to Kirja, and a few have even relocated from Joulu or neighboring villages. We have welcomed each family with open arms, hosting them at least once for a dinner at our place.

Watching my mates happily embrace this new lifestyle with me is the most gratifying experience of my life.

Today, Natalie, Jasper, and I got up way before dawn to quietly walk through the sleepy village. We stop in front of each and every house so I can sprinkle a fresh layer of snow for them to wake up to. For homes with young children, I add in some plump snowmen—one for each child living there—hoping they might enjoy the extra surprise.

"I think this is my favorite house so far," Natalie whispers, coming to a stop in front of a creatively decorated home. The pathway is lined with giant candy canes as tall as Jasper, leading all the way to a front door with an elf-sized ginger-bread man propped up against it.

"Why doesn't that surprise me?" Jasper says softly, humor coloring his words. He stares at her with so much love, and I rub at my chest where the same emotion runs deep within me.

I strategically direct a flurry of snow onto the ginger-bread man, making him look like he's clad in a pink bikini.

"The kids are going to love that when they wake up," Natalie says and hooks her arm through mine, directing us to the last few houses remaining.

"I aim to please, princess." I place a kiss on her cheek and a shiver of glee vibrates down the bond.

Jasper's spontaneous nickname he gave Natalie at the beginning of the month has kind of stuck. Even though she rolled her eyes a couple of times or pretended she didn't care, the read we have on her real emotions is a clear indication that our woman likes to be given the regal treatment from time to time. She deserves nothing less.

Natalie is strong, brave, and unapologetic about her fierce love for us. However, underneath that tough shell is a heart so tender that we'll quite literally do anything to keep it safe.

"Talking about aiming to please," Jasper says, lacing his warm fingers with my icy ones before putting them in his coat pocket, "You guys ready to have a full house today?"

Natalie beams at us. "I am so ready. Quill's making his famous chicken pot pie, and Daddy Santa is roasting a big Christmas ham. If you add in our casseroles and salads, along with whatever the Alberad boys and their mates are bringing, I think we'll have more than enough for everyone."

I nod, mentally adding up all the people we're expecting. "Nick might still be tired after his busy night of deliveries, but he said he wanted to make some *joulutorttu* for dessert when he gets to Kirja this afternoon. I went ahead and prepped the puff pastry for him and got the prune jam and other ingredients so there won't be too much left to do. We can just help him fold the pastry into stars and pop them in the oven after dinner. They taste great fresh."

We stop in front of the final house and, just because I'm feeling so ridiculously joyful today, add a mini polar bear to their snowmen.

When we start walking again, Jasper slips his hand back into mine and lifts it to his mouth, blowing warm air over my cold fingers. "Bertie told me he's bringing stollen, which I've kindly requested he make, and I think Everett got something from a fancy Vegas place. Rollo is probably bringing some kind of meat."

Natalie turns and walks backward while talking. "I'm so excited to see the girls again. We text often, but to actually have Diana, Sadie, and Florence here will be so much fun! It sucks that the others from the island couldn't make it this time, maybe next year."

Jasper's smile turns sly. "It'll be interesting to see how Rollo and his brothers are with Diana. They're very tight-lipped about their situation, but I'm sure I can needle them enough to get some kind of answers."

"Oh, I'll be keeping a careful eye on the four of them too. I want to know how their dynamic works. Do you think she—"

I cut Natalie's rambling off as I fist the front of her coat and drag her into our arms. "You two are trouble."

"But you love trouble."

"I really do."

OUR HOUSE IS FULL. Busy. Chaotic. And I wouldn't have Christmas dinner any other way again.

The voices of fourteen people chatting blend with the clanking of utensils on plates as we finish up the most delicious dinner. Jazz carols play softly in the background, creating the perfect harmony to the cozy atmosphere.

For our Christmas meal, we wedged two tables together to create one large seating arrangement, covering it with a deep red cloth. A pine garland with glittering ornaments stretches down the center of the table, dotted with tall white candles Natalie had to have. She said something about it creating the right ambiance. Jasper added strings of twinkling lights and wove them around the center arrangement, while I stacked plates with festive napkins.

On my left, Nick smiles at the story Quill tells him about his latest ice-fishing experience. My brother gives each person his full attention, despite how exhausted he must be after a full night of work.

The two sisters, Sadie and Florence, have an animated discussion across from me. One sister is dressed in a sparkly top that resembles the silver ornaments on the tree behind her, the other in a quirky hand-knit sweater with an oak tree on the front. It's endearing to watch two people so completely opposite lean into each other, holding hands whenever they can, while still keeping some part of their bodies connected to their mates next to them.

At the other end of the dining table, my father gently engages the wolf shifters in conversation, even if their attention keeps diverting back to Diana. He has grown out his beard since we reconnected, once again embracing his Santa heritage.

Jasper places a hand on my thigh, and says into my mind, *"Are you also enjoying how obsessed the wolf brothers are with Diana?"*

I take the last bite of my food, then put my knife and fork together. *"They're almost as bad as I am. I'm more than obsessed with you and Natalie."*

"Stop," Natalie says with gentle remonstrance as she nods along to whatever Diana is telling her. *"You're making me horny and some of these monsters have super sniffers. So unless you're planning to eat some sugar cookies for dessert, then you're going to have to stop saying things that'll make me drip."*

Jasper smothers a laugh and I cough, drawing everyone's gazes to us. I quickly recover and raise my glass. "How about a toast?"

Everyone follows suit and raises their glasses.

"To the happiest Christmas ever."

"To the happiest Christmas ever," they repeat, clinking glasses and exchanging sentimental looks that mirror my own.

After dinner, our guests retire to the living room for coffee and pastries. I watch them mingle from the kitchen doorway, silently basking in the beauty of so many loved ones from such different backgrounds coming together today. In *our* home.

I mentally capture the image, knowing no camera can do it justice and not ever wanting to forget this sight, or this feeling.

Next to the giant Christmas tree, sent straight from Pehmolelu—with an abundance of ornaments included—Jasper sits in an armchair with Natalie in his lap. I don't think anyone has noticed yet, but the garlands Natalie hung in the tree aren't festive flags. They're cutouts of our cocks that she traced onto felt for accuracy.

A snort escapes me when I realize she's draped them strategically, placing two balls below each cock.

Nick joins me and leans against the opposite doorjamb, a serene smile on his face as he also takes in the sight of our full and festive living room.

"This is my favorite Christmas ever," he says, turning that sweet smile on me.

"Me too. Thanks for coming."

"Thanks for inviting me." The genuine gratitude in his voice makes my heart so full, and I thank the fates for bringing us all together.

Needing to change the subject before I get emotional, I ask, "How did deliveries go? Checked your list twice?"

"I wouldn't be Santa if I didn't," Nick says with a shy smile, his cheeks brightening with a blush. He clears his throat and turns serious. "Cole, Christmas cheer was much higher than usual this year, and I think we can expect the trend to continue now that we're done with coal for the Naughty List."

"That's wonderful news, Nick. I really do hope the books make a difference."

"I think they already are."

"Yeah?"

"Let me show you. But call your mates over too, I think they'd like to see it."

"Jas, Nat, can you come over here? Nick wants to show us something."

Jasper and Natalie get up without needing any further explanation, and make their way over to us, hand in hand.

Nick shakes his head and lets out a sigh full of longing. "That's one neat trick. I've started praying to the fates that they send me someone special, too. Seeing you this happy makes me believe there's a mate somewhere out there for me."

Natalie lays a hand on Nick's shoulder. "I definitely believe so. They'll show up when you least expect it."

Jasper comes to stand behind me and pulls me into his front. "Wouldn't that be funny, though? If someone just appears out of nowhere and falls into your lap?"

"I can only dream," Nick says wistfully, his eyes glazing over with a faraway look.

I raise my brows at him. "Never say never."

Nick blinks as if to clear the thoughts from his head and takes out his phone. "So, technically there aren't any rules against it, but I took a picture that I *have* to show you. There was this one boy who woke up just as I left. He's on the Naughty List and I could see he didn't expect to find anything under the tree for him. But when he found a parcel with his name on it, he instantly unwrapped it and started reading your book."

Nick winces before continuing. "This is probably where I should say something about how he should've waited until morning to open presents with the rest of the household, and how that probably contributed to him being on the Naughty List, but…"

Nick holds out his phone and we gather around it, staring at the picture of a boy completely engrossed in a book. *Our* book.

Rubbing at his beard, Nick says, "I shouldn't have risked sticking around longer than was strictly necessary, but I just had to show you. He got lost in that book. Read it from start to finish, and he's not even an avid reader."

The smile stretching across Jasper's face is absolutely breathtaking. "Wow. He looks… captivated."

A single tear tracks down Natalie's cheek, her lip wobbling with emotion. "He likes our book."

"Cole, Jasper, Natalie—what you're doing for the children is going to affect them for the rest of their lives. Thank you."

I wipe at my eyes, feeling an immense amount of pride for my family well up in me. "I'm just so happy to be part of your team, Nick. Working together to make the world a slightly better place is pretty rewarding. And doing it all with my mates, and my brother at my side… Thank you."

Nick places his hand on my shoulder, and after a moment's hesitation pulls me into a bear hug. He breathes in deeply, and on the exhale whispers, "Brothers."

We step back and hold each other's eyes for a moment, before a bashful smile tilts Nick's mouth up. "Can I give you your Christmas present now?"

"Sure. I thought we'd exchange presents later, but we can do that now if you want."

"Let's do everyone else's later. I'd like to give just yours now, if that's okay?"

"Yeah, of course." My heart hammers in my chest as Nick walks over to his magic Santa bag next to the tree. He grabs a small box lying right near the front like it was waiting for him.

Behind me, Jasper goes still and our bond floods with gratefulness and appreciation and love, like he somehow knows what's inside. Natalie senses the emotions too and places her hand on my lower back, shoring me up with her presence and support as Nick comes back and places the box in my hands.

I quickly unwrap the present and flip the lid before a single sob tears from me.

I'm absolutely speechless. My eyes well up as I look to my brother with immense appreciation for the significant gift he's given me.

Tears form in Nick's eyes and his cheeks turn a ruddy color. "I'm sorry I didn't think of this sooner, but I contacted

Adelbert to have a glamour ring made for you. You're free to travel anywhere in the world while blending in looking human. Maybe you can go visit Jasper's parents in the Alps, or even go meet Natalie's mom in Arizona."

"How about my Christmas-elf side keeping me bound to the Arctic?"

"I had that taken care of too. There are no restrictions around you, no magic keeping you here. You're free to come and go with your mates as you please. But I hope you always come back. I'd really like to have my brother close."

As one, we surge forward and sandwich Nick between us, squeezing him with all our love as we rain words of thanks down on him.

When we finally step back, we're all wiping at the happy tears streaming down our faces. It's not like we *want* to leave Kirja, but having that option—that freedom—is very liberating. And a vacation somewhere warm sounds like a really good plan.

"Thanks Nick. You've done so much for us. How about you go relax by the fire, and I'll bring you a glass of milk?" Jasper suggests in a whisper. I'm afraid his normal voice will probably break from all the emotion it still carries.

"Yes, please. That would be lovely," Nick says wetly, dabbing at his eyes with his handkerchief.

"I'll bring you some of those delicious pastries you made. The next batch should be cooled down now," Natalie adds, her voice the first to return to a stable condition.

Nick smiles and heads off to the giant armchair we had ordered to fit his large Santa frame, while we prepare his drink and a plate of *joulutorttu* for him, and another plate for us.

All our guests are spread out around the festive living room, decorated with nutcrackers, stockings, and of course, mistletoe. A few chat in a small cluster, some discuss the snowmen outside that I created to represent each person here, and others cuddle up on couches. It's cozy and absolutely perfect.

I put Nick's plate on the coffee table next to his chair, and hand him his glass. He digs into his first pastry as I join Jasper and Natalie on the two-seater couch, sandwiching her between us, before we feed each other bites of plum pastries.

Something rustles in Nick's Santa bag, and my hand stops halfway to my mouth. The whole house stills as all the males go on high alert.

A human woman crawls out of the bag, takes one look at us and sprints toward the door, only to back up again when she sees the others standing in her way. She gapes at us wide-eyed and panicked, her gaze bouncing from Jasper's horns to my ears to Bertie to Everett, then settles on the pack of wolves forming a protective barrier around Diana. They must have shifted the moment they sensed danger.

The stranger takes careful steps backward as low growls rumble from their throats. She doesn't break eye contact with them and she lifts her hands. "I come in peace. I swear. I just…"

Her heel catches on Nick's foot and she stumbles back. Nick's hands instinctively go out to steady her, spilling his milk as the woman falls directly into his lap.

Jasper snorts. "Told you that could happen."

Christmas wishes really do come true.

ACKNOWLEDGMENTS

Thank you so much for reading Courting the Krampus and joining Natalie, Jasper, and Cole on their journey to a happily ever after. If you're curious about some of the other couples, you can read about Sadie and Everett in Tempting the Dhampir, or Florence and Adelbert in Enchanting the Elf. More stories are coming soon!

If you enjoyed this book, please consider leaving a rating and review. They're the lifeline of indie authors and will help me gain some much needed visibility in the wonderful world of monster romance.

None of my books are complete without the incredible support of some special people, and I'd like to take a moment to thank them for helping me get this book into your hands.

Adrienne, thank you for all the brainstorming sessions and indulging my weirdness. When we sat in that park in Seoul and I explained scenes I had planned for this book until we were both red in the face… Thank you for loving me regardless (or maybe even more because of it). You're the bestest of best friends and an integral part of the Alberad world.

T.B. Wiese, you're the gift who keeps giving. Thank you for all the encouragement and helping me finetune the big and small plot points. I still insist that none of my characters have runny noses in the cold, despite them quite literally living in the North Pole. Magic helps.

Mon Reyes, you always understand my characters so well. You knocked it out of the park once again with Cole, Natalie, and Jasper.

Colette, thank you my dear friend for your beautiful typography and design on this cover. Thank you also for listening to my countless ramblings and chatting me through difficult parts when I got stuck.

My street team—McKayala, Laura, Kara, Monika, Lindsey, Michelle, Katie, Melanie, Josie, Micheala, Katie B, Erin, and Monica. Thank you, thank you, thank you. Thank you for supporting me and caring about my characters and the stories I write. You are so dear to me and I treasure each of you.

To my husband, who is my favorite human, thank you for supporting me, and thank you for pushing me to take breaks when I don't even know I need them. You're the ultimate book boyfriend.

And to the real MVP: *you*, dear reader. Thank you for choosing this book and giving my characters your time and attention. I truly appreciate you <3

—Elle

P.S. I'd love to hear from you, so please don't hesitate to contact me.

ALSO BY ELLE STERLING

Tempting the Dhampir

Enchanting the Elf

Courting the Krampus

ABOUT THE AUTHOR

Elle Sterling is a monster and paranormal author based in South Korea.

Her stories are fun and flirty, filled with heart and spice. HEAs guaranteed.

Much like her own life after emigrating from South Africa, she enjoys writing characters crossing cultural barriers and loving without restraint.

You can usually find Elle in her writing cave with coffee within reach at all times. She also enjoys grilled kimchi-and-cheese sandwiches and hibernates during the humid summer until the weather has cooled.

Elle loves connecting with readers, so visit her at the links below or email her elle@ellesterling.com

www.ingramcontent.com/pod-product-compliance
Lightning Source LLC
Chambersburg PA
CBHW021153160726
47994CB00001B/193